ABOUT THE AUTHOR

Barbara Hall has written several award-winning young adult novels. As well as *The House Across the Cove*, published by Hodder Children's Books for younger readers, she is also the author of two adult novels, *A Better Place* and *Closer to Home*. She has written and produced many television dramas, including *Northern Exposure* and *Chicago Hope*. Barbara lives in Los Angeles with her daughter, Faith.

Cloudburst

Barbara Hall

*Hodder
Children's
Books*

a division of Hodder Headline plc

For my brother and his family,
with special thanks to Robin

One

The summer my nephew Bodean turned nine he started driving me crazy. Up till then he'd been a pretty good kid. I didn't mind playing games with him and taking him for long walks around the farm. I always liked the idea of having a nephew. It was as if I'd gotten a head start in life. By the time I was five I was already someone's aunt.

Bodean never called me 'aunt.' He went around telling folks I was his sister or his cousin. Papa said he was just too young to understand the family hierarchy, but I figured he just didn't want to give me the upper hand.

I don't know what came over him that summer. He was all the time back-talking me and telling me to shut up. But the worst part was he had picked up all these crazy sayings like 'Do me a favor' and 'Make me an offer.' I didn't know what they meant, and I don't think he did either, but he sure was fond of them.

I clearly remember the day he started getting feisty, or at least the day I first noticed it. It was Saturday afternoon, the middle of July, and I was trying to fix lunch. He was dancing around the kitchen, popping my legs with a dishtowel.

1

'Go on, Bodean,' I said. 'I'm trying to cut this corn bread even.'

He said, 'Make me an offer.'

'All right. Go on before I slap you senseless.'

'Do me a favor.'

'I'm gonna tell your daddy on you.'

He stopped and weighed the importance of that threat. His daddy was my older brother, Flood. Flood was kind of inconsistent in his discipline of Bodean. Sometimes he was real tough on him and other times he'd let him get away with murder. Since it was a Saturday, Flood was probably planning to go to the pool hall after he got through working in the field. That put him in a good mood and Bodean knew it.

So Bodean said, 'Go ahead and tell. Tattle tattle, here comes the cattle.'

'I'm gonna knock you sapwinded.'

'Do me a favor.'

I just let it go at that. There was no arguing with Bodean. Papa said all his problems came from the fact he didn't have a proper mother. Flood's wife Becky left when he was only three. I never was sure why, and Flood doesn't like to discuss it to this day.

That was one thing me and Bodean had in common. Neither one of us had a mother. At least Bodean's mother was alive somewhere. Mine died when I was born. I was what they call a 'change of life' baby. The doctor told Mama she shouldn't risk having another one, but she put her foot down because her whole life she had wanted to have a daughter. Well, she got her wish. I was (and still am) a girl.

Sometimes I think I'm luckier than Bodean in a way. Mama didn't want to leave me; she just didn't have a whole lot of choice in the matter. But with Becky, it's hard to say. She didn't have to leave and she could have taken Bodean with her. She did have a choice. Papa said when Bodean got older he would spend a lot of time wondering about that.

He was already starting to wonder a little. He went through a spell of asking me questions about her. I tried to remember the best I could. I was only his age when she left. But I knew she was pretty and talked in a quiet voice. She sang all the time. When Becky was around there always seemed to be music in the house. Then one day it just stopped.

Bodean didn't ask about his mama after he turned nine. He was too interested in making smart remarks.

'That corn bread's all crooked,' he said, standing on his tiptoes.

'It wouldn't be if you'd let me alone.'

'You can't cook. Nobody's gonna marry you.'

I was about to give him a swat on the behind when the back door opened and Flood came in. He stomped his feet on the mat and coughed. His clothes were soaked with sweat, and his blond hair was matted down under his John Deere cap. Flood was a real fan of John Deere machinery.

He could get downright indignant about it. One of the current rifts in the house was that my father had tried to save money by buying a tractor that wasn't a John Deere. Flood cursed and shouted and sulked for a week. He still hadn't fully recovered.

'Hey, Dad,' Bodean said, 'Dutch cut the corn bread all crooked.'

Flood lit a cigarette and said, 'Get away from that stove before you burn yourself.'

Bodean pouted. One thing he hadn't counted on was if things were going bad with the crop, Flood would be cranky even if it was a Saturday. Bodean was at a loss what to do now. He liked to act tough around his daddy, but he didn't want to risk a scolding. More than anything in the world he wanted to please Flood, but he hadn't worked out exactly how to accomplish that.

Flood went to the refrigerator and started gulping iced tea out of the pitcher. I'd long ago stopped telling him not to do that. It's a well-known fact around here that you can't tell Flood Peyton a thing. He's as hard-headed as they come.

'Where's Macy?' Flood asked, picking at the fried chicken and burning his fingers. He let out a yelp and shook his hand. Bodean giggled nervously.

'Lying down. She's got a headache from the heat.'

'She's always got a pain somewhere.'

That wasn't true, really. It was only the heat that made Aunt Macy feel bad. She was fine in the winter.

'Where's Papa?' I asked.

'Out there moping.'

'What for?'

'Don't look good. Crop's drying up, and there ain't a sign of rain.'

'We gonna lose it?'

'Might,' he said and dumped his cigarette ashes in the sink. When Flood walked into a room it became his, like no one else was even there.

'I told him not to buy that piece of junk for a tractor.'

I frowned at him. 'That tractor don't have a thing to do with whether it rains or not.'

'Bad luck is what it is.'

He was real superstitious about things like that. Most farmers were. My papa wasn't, though. He said, 'You can always find something to blame besides yourself.' I figured that was pretty true.

Bodean was getting tired of being ignored, so he piped up, 'Hey, Dad, when you gonna take me hunting?'

'I just took you last spring.'

'Aw, that was dumb old grouse. I wanna get me a deer.'

Bodean made a rifle with his arms and pretended to shoot at something, but Flood just laughed.

'You ain't big enough to get a deer. More likely a deer'd get you.'

I had to giggle, even though I knew it would make Bodean mad. He hated to be teased about being little. He was about the right size for his age, but he was in a big hurry to be a grownup. Flood looked at me and winked.

5

'A deer'd probably eat you for dinner,' he went on.

Bodean said, 'Do me a favor.'

Two

Papa finally came in, Aunt Macy came down from her nap, and we had lunch. Bodean had settled down considerably. He was still nursing a pout, and he always got a little quiet around Papa. My father was generally a patient man, but he didn't put up with foolishness from anybody, least of all from a nine-year-old.

Papa seemed tired but he resisted talking about his troubles. He said it wasn't a good idea to discuss bad news at the table. Flood was sulky, and Aunt Macy wasn't eating much. She always lost her appetite in the summer.

She was my father's sister, and they looked a lot alike around the eyes. I got those eyes, too. A grayish color, deep set, turned down a little around the corners. 'Melancholy eyes,' Becky used to say, and for some reason that made me feel proud.

Aunt Macy moved in with us right after her second husband died, not long before Becky and Flood got married. She and Becky always got along real well together. But she and Flood were a different story. Flood made her nervous, and he seemed to enjoy picking on her. Flood was funny that way. He always found your weakness and went after it.

Papa said, 'This is the best fried chicken I ever had, Dutch.'

'I wish I could have helped more, but that headache came on all of a sudden,' said Aunt Macy.

'Always happens around mealtime, don't it?' Flood said.

Papa shot him a look and then said to me, 'Some of those tomatoes are ready for picking. You better get them before the birds get them.'

'I hate tomatoes,' Bodean announced.

'Nobody's gonna make you eat 'em,' Papa said, giving him a wink.

Bodean liked the sound of that and suddenly felt inspired to talk. 'When I grow up I'm never gonna eat another vegetable in my life.'

'What are you gonna eat?' Papa asked.

'Only what I like. Hamburgers and French fries.'

'French fries are vegetables, stupid,' I said.

'They are not.'

'They are, too. They're potatoes.'

'If you don't eat your vegetables now you're never going to grow up,' said Aunt Macy, indicating the untouched green beans on his plate. Bodean looked sorry he'd ever mentioned it.

Flood pushed his plate back and lit a cigarette. Papa didn't like smoking at the table, but he didn't say anything.

'Flood, I forgot to tell you, somebody called you today,' Aunt Macy said. 'A girl. I think it was Lucy Cabbot.'

I looked at Flood. He was sucking ice cubes out of his tea.

8

'She sure is a nice girl,' Papa said. Flood wouldn't even look at him.

Lucy was this woman about Flood's age who always talked to him at church. Flood didn't seem too impressed by her. I was glad of that. It made me feel uncomfortable to see Flood with any woman except Becky.

'She's right pretty, too,' Papa added. Flood looked up.

'I don't see anything special about her.'

'Maybe you're not looking hard enough,' said Papa.

'Maybe you ought to stop trying to marry me off.'

The table got quiet. Everybody stared at their plates.

'We sure could use some rain,' Aunt Macy said finally, and I wished she hadn't because the mention of rain made wrinkles grow across Papa's forehead.

'Better get some soon,' Flood said. 'Tobacco leaves are already starting to shrivel up, only 'bout half the size they need to be. And we still owe on that tractor.'

Flood was looking at Papa while he said all this, but Papa wouldn't look back at him. He just pressed his lips together and reached for another piece of chicken.

Nobody talked for a minute, then finally Papa said, 'We've had worse summer's than this.'

'I'd like to know when,' Flood challenged.

'I'll tell you when. Summer right after you were born. Didn't rain for two solid months and we still made a profit.'

Flood huffed. 'We haven't made a profit since I can remember.'

'Hard to make money on a farm anymore. 'Bout all you

can do is break even. Make enough money to pay off your debts from the year before.'

'So sell the thing,' Flood grumbled. 'If you ask me, it's a big white elephant.'

To my surprise Papa chuckled. 'Always seems like that in a drought, doesn't it? No, I won't sell this farm. My great-grandfather managed to hang on to it all through the Civil War. I'm not gonna let it go because of a little dry weather.'

'I'd rather shave my head than eat a tomato,' Bodean said, wanting the conversation to get back to him, but all he did was remind Aunt Macy that he still hadn't touched his green beans. She told him he couldn't leave the table till he did.

Flood just scowled at the wall, and I sat there feeling myself getting mad at him. I always got mad when he tried to pick a fight with Papa. He seemed to enjoy it. Aunt Macy said it was because they were too much alike, both hard-headed in different directions.

When Papa had finished eating he pushed his plate back and reached for a toothpick. He swirled it around in his mouth for a while, then looked at me.

'Dutch, I got some news for you. We're gonna have some company soon, next day or so, and I'm gonna have to ask you to share your room.'

'What kind of company?' I asked.

'Girl, about your age. Little older, maybe. She's your cousin, Norma. Eugene's daughter.'

I'd never met my cousin Norma, or my Uncle Eugene for that matter, but secretly I'd always wondered about them. They were sort of like a legend in our family.

Uncle Eugene wasn't held in high esteem. Papa hadn't spoken to him in years. The trouble all started when Papa went off to fight in the Korean War. Uncle Eugene was supposed to stay behind and help with the farm; instead he took off to the city. He got out of the army on a farm deferment and then just left, which was a pretty rotten thing to do. My grandpa had to manage all by himself, and to this day Aunt Macy swears that was what sent him to an early grave.

Uncle Eugene struck it rich in the city, working in a bank. He got married late in life and had this one daughter, Norma, not long before Mama had me. When I was young I pretended sometimes that Norma was my twin. In my imagination she looked exactly like me and had all the same thoughts as me, even though we had never met.

'What's she coming for?' I asked, trying not to sound excited.

'Eugene and Fran are having some problems,' Papa answered, 'and they just want to send her away while they get things settled.'

'What kind of problems?'

'Marital,' Aunt Macy said in a low voice.

'Well, that's just what we need around here,' said Bodean. 'Another stinking girl.'

'Watch out, boy,' Papa said in a stern voice, but Flood had actually laughed at Bodean's remark, and that made him feel brave.

11

'I hope she can cook better than Dutch,' said Bodean. Papa let that one go.

'I hope you don't mind, Dutch. It won't be for long.'

'I don't mind,' I said, still not sure how excited I should sound. I didn't want Papa to think I was approving of Uncle Eugene.

Flood finished his cigarette and stubbed it out in his leftover mashed potatoes. Aunt Macy frowned with distaste.

'Oh, Flood. I wish you wouldn't do that.'

'If you don't like it, don't look at it.'

The next thing I knew, Papa picked up his fork and speared it in the table, barely missing Flood's hand. My mouth dropped open and Aunt Macy sucked in a breath. Flood just lifted his eyes slowly to Papa.

Papa said, 'Don't you ever talk like that to a woman in my presence.'

Flood slid his chair back and walked out, slamming the back door behind him. The rest of us stayed quiet. Papa just shook his head.

'That boy's got the devil in him,' he said.

Bodean grinned. He thought that was a compliment.

Three

In case you haven't guessed, my real name isn't Dutch. It's Margaret. People have called me Dutch all my life, though, and I don't mind because I don't like my real name much better.

My grandfather was the one who started calling me Dutch. The story goes that when I was little I was always speaking jibberish, and Grandpa said when I opened my mouth it sounded like I was speaking Dutch. I don't remember very much about him so I just have to take everybody's word for it.

Somehow the name just stuck, and even my friends at school call me that. The teachers tried to call me Margaret, but it never caught my attention so they just gave up.

Bodean isn't his real name, either. I guess it is in a way – it's a combination of both his names. Robert Dean Peyton. Becky used to call him Bobby Dean. That's what she wanted everybody else to call him, too, and we did while she was around. Flood gave him the nickname, even though Becky hated it. After she left there was nobody around to fuss at Flood when he said 'Bodean,' so we all just went along with it.

Flood is just Flood. That's what my mother named him because the night he was born there was a flash flood in Marston, the town where we live. The roads were all washed out and Mama couldn't even get to a hospital, so she had Flood right there in her bedroom, with the help of some neighbors. She was so overwhelmed by the whole experience that she couldn't even think of a proper name for him. She just kept calling him her flood baby; then it was Flood, and then suddenly it was his name.

There hasn't been a real flood in Marston since that night. There hasn't been anything very exciting in Marston since I can remember. Once the town hall burned down, but I was just a baby and missed all the commotion.

It's not really fair to call Marston a town. It doesn't even show up on most maps of Virginia. It's a tiny dot in the middle of the state, almost on the North Carolina line. It's far away from everything exciting, if there is anything exciting in Virginia, which I wouldn't really know firsthand. Papa always said that Richmond, the state capital, was a nice place and he promised to take me there one day. But I think he wanted to avoid it because that was where Uncle Eugene lived.

Marston is mostly farmland. You can drive all over and just see rows and rows of tobacco and corn. There's one stoplight on Main Street, and they put that up only last year. There are a few shops, a courthouse, a pool hall, a diner, a drugstore, and a grocery market. We don't have any big supermarkets or malls or movie theaters. Not much to do after dark except ride around, which was what all the kids did when they got their drivers' licenses. On a Friday night the whole town seemed to rumble from the car engines, and quick bursts of music from the radios echoed down the streets.

Sometimes I wished I lived in a bigger place, but most times I was pretty satisfied. There was plenty of room to ride a bike or walk through the woods. And everybody in town knew each other. Aunt Macy said when I got older I wouldn't think of that as an advantage, but I had yet to work out the meaning of that.

Papa always said you should never be ashamed of your home or your town. When you are, then you're getting too big for your britches. But in the days leading up to Norma's arrival I started to get a little worried about what she might think of the place.

I cleaned the house nine times over. I kept having to pick up after Bodean because he left his toy trucks and guns scattered from one end to the other. I put the best sheets on the spare bed in my room, and I went down to the dime store and spent my allowance on some pictures to hang on the walls. They weren't anything special, just roses and daises, but I thought they might brighten the room up a little.

I also bought some lip gloss and mascara. I was sure Norma wore makeup, and I didn't want her to think I was completely out of it. I imagined myself saying to her, 'Here, Norma, you want to try some of my lip gloss?' I just couldn't wait to say that to her.

While I was in town buying things I ran into two boys I knew from school, Kenny Wells and Ethan Cole. They were both a year older than me, but I knew them pretty well because their families belonged to my church. Kenny and Ethan were at the age where they didn't bother to come to church anymore except on special occasions, but when we were little we used to play freeze tag on the church lawn before the service started. I'd known those boys all my life and now they'd grown up to be good-looking and popular. All the girls got weak-kneed when Kenny walked by. He was just plain movie star material. Blond hair and brown eyes with a natural tan and long legs. He walked around like he owned the world, and in a way I guess he did.

Ethan wasn't quite as cute but he was popular just by being Kenny's friend. To be honest, I liked Ethan a lot better than Kenny. I liked his red hair and his blue eyes, and the sound of his laugh. He grinned a lot and when he did his eyes squinted till they were nearly shut. Most girls thought that made him look goofy, but I didn't.

He and Kenny were sitting on the courthouse steps drinking Cokes. Kenny called out, 'Hey, Dutch! Where you been keeping yourself?'

I tucked my bag of belongings under my arm and walked over there. 'What are y'all doing?'

'What's it look like we're doing?' Kenny was the sarcastic type. He always sounded pleased with himself.

'Looks like you're wasting time,' I said, and Ethan grinned.

'You talk like a train hit you,' Kenny said. 'I been

working in tobacco every blame day since school let out.'

'Congratulations,' I said. The best thing to do with Kenny was play his own game. He respected you for it.

'What're you buying?' Ethan asked.

'Oh, nothing.'

Kenny grabbed the bag from me and started looking through my purchases. He held one of the framed pictures up in the sunlight and laughed.

'Well, if that ain't a masterpiece.'

'I never said it was,' I replied, snatching it back.

'I didn't know you were into art, Dutch.'

I felt my cheeks burn a little, but I told myself to forget it because once people got popular they were obligated to act like jerks. It was some kind of unwritten rule.

Now Kenny had discovered my mascara and was fiddling with it.

'Who are you making yourself beautiful for?' he asked.

'Nobody.'

I looked at Ethan. He was busy dumping some salted peanuts into his Coke bottle.

Kenny handed my stuff back to me and yawned. I figured it was time to say something interesting because they both looked a little bored.

'I'm having company,' I said. 'My cousin Norma's coming to visit. From Richmond.'

'How old is she?' Kenny asked.

' 'Bout your age.'

'Good looking?'

'I don't know. I never met her.'

Ethan looked up then. 'You've got a cousin you never met?'

'I told you, she lives in Richmond,' I said as a defense. I didn't want to get into the whole family business.

'Richmond's not that far away,' Kenny challenged, but luckily Ethan interrupted him.

'When's she coming?'

'Tomorrow.'

'Bring her around to our softball game.'

'Well,' I said, 'I'm sure that's the *first* thing she'll want to do.'

Ethan laughed and Kenny just shook his head.

'You got a smart mouth on you, Dutch.'

'I was born with it,' I said with a shrug. 'I reckon I'll see you guys later.'

As I turned away Kenny got one last shot in.

'It's too bad some other parts of you aren't as developed as your mouth.'

I blushed like mad and looked down at my chest without meaning to. It was a real sensitive issue with me. I was still about as flat-chested as the day I was born. Aunt Macy said I was a late bloomer. But try explaining that to someone like Kenny.

I just kept walking, pretending I didn't hear him.

Flood picked me up on the corner next to the grocery store. When I got in the truck he said, 'What's wrong with you? Your face is beet red.'

'Sunburn, I guess.'

I leaned my head against the window. Kenny and Ethan were probably still laughing about me, punching each other's ribs the way guys do, stomping their tennis shoes on the ground.

Or even worse, they'd probably already forgotten about me.

Four

The next day around noon Papa went to the bus station to pick up Norma. He asked if I wanted to go with him, but I said no. I told him I had too much work to do. That wasn't really the truth. I just didn't think it would look good to be hanging idly around the bus station when Norma arrived. I wanted her to think that her visit was just another event in my full and busy life.

The only chore I had left to do was shucking corn. It was my least favorite job in the world, but I figured if I did it while I was waiting for her to come it wouldn't seem so bad. I brought the bag of corn out on the front porch and planned to put it away as soon as I saw Papa's truck coming down the road.

I tried to get Bodean to help me, but he was afraid of corn worms, even if he wouldn't admit it. He just said, 'I ain't touching a vegetable. No, sir, that's ladies' work.'

He stayed on the front porch while I shucked, shooting hickory nuts out of the tree with his BB gun. Aunt Macy came out onto the porch and looked off down the road.

'Any sign of them yet?' she asked.

'Not yet.'

'I reckon the bus is late,' she said and went back in the house.

After a while Bodean turned to me and said, 'Do you think my daddy's handsome?'

'Of course I don't. He's my brother.'

Bodean puzzled over that. He didn't like to think of Flood as being my brother. He especially didn't like to think of him as being Papa's son. That meant Papa could officially tell him what to do, and Bodean didn't favor that a bit. I reckon he liked to think Flood just dropped into the world of his own accord.

'I heard some girls at church saying he was handsome,' Bodean went on. 'They said he was the best catch around.'

'Well, they shouldn't have been talking like that at church.' I paused to consider if Flood was really handsome. He had a rough look about him, and it seemed to me he was always frowning. He was big and tall and looked like someone you wouldn't want to make mad. He had blond hair, which turned even blonder in the summer. Everyone said he looked like Mama, and from the pictures I'd seen of her it was true. He got her eyes, a clear, crystal blue. I supposed when he got cleaned up for a night on the town he looked all right.

'Your mama thought he was handsome,' I said.

Bodean huffed. 'She wasn't no good.'

I bristled. 'Where'd you hear that kind of talk?'

'Daddy.'

'I can't believe he said that.'

'He said any woman who'd run off and leave her family was no count to start out with. And that's what she did, isn't it?'

'Well,' I said carefully, 'maybe she had her reasons.'

'So how come she never wrote to me?'

That was a real good question and one I didn't like to think about very much. I had a hard enough time excusing Becky for running away. I always told myself I couldn't blame her because I didn't know the facts. But it did seem a little strange that she never tried to write or call. She acted like Bodean didn't even exist.

The reason I didn't like to think about that question was that there were only two real answers to it, and neither one made me very comfortable. One was that something bad had happened to her. Maybe she had died or something. I never really knew anyone who died, so that was hard to accept. But the other answer was even worse – she just didn't care. And if she didn't care about Bodean, then what he said was probably true. She was no good.

The question made me cross because I couldn't answer it. I was trying to think of something wise to say when I saw Papa's truck coming down the road. I stuffed the corn back into the bag and hid it behind the rocking chair. I wiped my hands on my shorts, ran my fingers through my hair, and took a deep breath. Bodean scrambled to his feet, aiming his BB gun at the truck.

'Put that thing away,' I said, swatting at him. 'You're gonna put somebody's eye out.'

'It's empty. I run out of BB's.'

'Still, do you want Norma to think you're a hooligan?'

'I don't care what an old girl thinks of me.'

The truck came to a stop in front of the house. Papa got out, then went around and opened the other door. After what seemed like forever, Norma stepped out.

I had an assortment of pictures in my mind as to what Norma would look like, but all of them were completely wrong. Part of me still believed she would look exactly like me, but I knew in my heart that wasn't realistic. Another part of me thought she would look exotic, like some woman from history . . . Cleopatra, maybe, with thick, square-cut hair and black eyes. And some small corner of my mind that always allowed for disaster pictured her as plain, even ugly, with buckteeth and freckles.

She was none of those things. She was blonde, but her hair was the color of straw, with dark streaks running through it. It fell past her shoulders and was tucked casually behind her ears, with one thick piece sweeping over her eyes. Her skin was porcelain white, like it would be cool and smooth to the touch. Her lips were broad with a pale pink shine. She wore long, dangling earrings, stonewashed jeans, a big white T-shirt with a belt around the waist, and sandals. She looked very well put together.

As she walked around the truck she stumbled a little but quickly recovered, tucking the loose piece of hair behind her ear and smiling at the ground, as if it had played a trick on her. When I saw that it made my heart jolt because right

24

then and there I knew who she was. She was the kind of girl who could trip on the sidewalk, laugh all the way down, and make you look stupid for standing up.

I stood still as a rock as they walked up to the porch. When they got close to me, she smiled. She had the straightest, whitest teeth I had ever seen. And I couldn't get over those earrings. They were silver triangles with black stones in them, swinging lazily below her chin.

Papa said, 'Dutch, this is your cousin, Norma Peyton.'

'Hi,' she said.

'Hi,' I answered.

Then, remembering my manners, I held out my hand and said, 'How do you do?'

She stared at my hand for a moment before she shook it. Her fingers were thin and smooth.

I looked at Bodean and saw that he had fallen in love with her. That was pretty obvious by the way his mouth was drooping open.

'This is my nephew, Bodean,' I said.

'That's a nice name,' she said.

'It ain't my real name,' Bodean said, almost apologetically. I'd never heard him admit that to anyone. But that was the effect that Norma had.

'I hope you had a pleasant trip,' I said. I had been practicing that line since I heard she was coming, but now it just sounded foolish.

'Oh, you know how bus trips are. Long and hot.' She sighed and I just nodded, even though I'd never been on a bus in my life except for a school bus.

Aunt Macy came out then, wiping her hands on her apron.

'This is your Aunt Macy,' Papa said to Norma.

'Glad to have you with us,' Aunt Macy said, smiling shyly at her.

'Well, thank you for having me.'

'I'll take your bags up,' Papa said.

'I'll help you,' Aunt Macy said. 'Dutch, there's a fresh pitcher of iced tea in the kitchen. Maybe Norma would like some.'

'That would be great,' said Norma.

We went into the kitchen, and I noticed my hands were shaking as I poured her tea. I had cut some mint from the garden that morning and I put a little sprig inside her glass. She sat down at the kitchen table and let out a sigh. Bodean was crouched in the corner, looking at her.

'Oh, that's cute,' she said about the mint when I put her glass down in front of her. She took small, noiseless sips.

I inspected her face while she drank. At first glance it looked like she wasn't wearing any makeup. But close up you could see she had gone to a lot of trouble to make herself look natural. The smooth white look of her skin was really a pale coat of makeup, and that soft pink glow in her cheeks was just the slightest touch of blush. Her lashes had been painted so delicately with mascara that you could practically count them.

She looked up at me, and my eyes darted away.

'We're gonna share a room,' I said. 'I hope you don't mind.'

'Not at all.'

I sat down at the table and looked around the kitchen, wondering what she thought of it. It was as clean as a pin but wasn't too fancy. She didn't seem to mind, though. She just kept sipping her tea and smiling at me.

'There's not much to do around here,' I said. 'We can go swimming and ride bikes. Then there's this softball team that plays on Wednesdays and weekends.' I cut myself off because I heard how I sounded – all eager and nervous.

'Softball?' she repeated, as if wondering what that meant. Then she said, 'I'm not too good at that.'

'No, we wouldn't play. We'd just watch it. I can't play either. I mean, I can but I'm not any good. It's just these guys who play . . .' And again I stopped myself before I sounded too much like an idiot. I wasn't sure what it was about her that made me babble. Maybe it was just that she was so calm and sure of herself. She made me feel out of control, like a bicycle with a wobbly wheel.

She took a long sip of tea, then said, 'Is your boyfriend on this softball team?'

I giggled in spite of myself. 'No, not really. I mean I don't exactly have a boyfriend.'

'Really?' She sounded surprised.

'Well, I mean . . . nobody special. Do you?'

'Sort of. His name is Marshall. He wants to marry me but . . .' She shrugged. 'Do you want to see a picture?'

'Sure.'

She reached into her handbag and pulled out a wallet. It was red leather with her initials on it.

She handed me a snapshot of a dark-haired guy. He was wearing a football uniform and holding a helmet under his arm. Handsome was a mild word for what he was. He sure put Kenny Wells in his place.

'He's cute,' I said simply.

She nodded, taking it back and staring at it. 'I guess I love him. It's hard to tell sometimes. I mean, if you love somebody or not.'

'Yeah,' I said, trying to sound as if I knew.

'He's gonna go to college next year, so who knows what will happen.'

'How old is he?'

'Seventeen,' she said. 'Two years older than me. But that's a good age difference. Girls are two years more mature than boys, according to what I've read. How old are you?'

'Fourteen,' I said, wishing I could say almost fifteen, but that would have been a downright lie. I'd just turned fourteen in June.

Suddenly Bodean said, 'Can you cook?'

She looked at him as if she'd forgotten he was there.

'A little bit. I can make brown sugar pie. Would you like me to make you one while I'm here?'

He nodded dumbly, then said, 'Dutch can't cook a lick.'

I could have killed him. Instead, I just rolled my eyes at Norma and she laughed.

'It's true,' Bodean insisted. 'Daddy says there hasn't been a decent meal in this house since his mama died.'

That was the limit. As soon as I saw Flood I was going to give him a piece of my mind. He was filling that child up with a lot of nonsense.

'Who's his daddy?' Norma asked me.

'My brother. His name's Flood. You'll meet him at supper.'

'And who's your mama?' she asked Bodean.

'My mama's no good,' was his answer.

Norma cleared her throat and said, 'Well, I guess that's what I get for prying.'

I couldn't say anything. I was too busy planning how and when to give Bodean a walloping he'd never forget.

Five

Supper that night was a lively occasion. With a new person at the table we suddenly got the idea that our lives were very interesting. We told her stories about ourselves, and she smiled and laughed whenever it was appropriate.

'Did you ever pull tobacco?' Bodean asked her when he finally worked up the nerve to speak.

'No. I'm afraid I don't know very much about farming.'

'That's okay,' Flood said. 'We don't know much about farming, either.'

Everyone laughed at that. It felt good to hear Flood joking.

'What else do you grow here?' she asked.

'Tobacco's our main crop,' Flood said. 'It's the only one that makes money. Then we got corn and potatoes, butter beans and green beans, and a few tomatoes.'

'I hate tomatoes,' Bodean added, and he blushed when Norma smiled at him.

'Well, it must be real satisfying,' she said, 'growing your own food. I know I could never do it. I can't even remember to water the plants at home.'

We all laughed.

31

Flood said, 'I've always wanted to have a cattle ranch, myself. I'm a lot better with animals than I am with vegetables.'

He gave a quick look to Papa, but Papa just kept his eyes on his plate.

'I guess y'all get up before daybreak,' Norma said.

'Don't you know it,' Flood answered.

Papa said, 'I wouldn't have it any other way. It's the most beautiful time of day. The whole world looks better before everybody wakes up and starts trampling through it.' He gave Norma a smile, which she returned.

'Don't worry, you'll get used to farm life after a while,' Flood assured her.

'Well, I hope so,' she said with a sigh. Then she looked at me and said, 'I'm sure Dutch and I will find plenty to do.'

I smiled, and she gave me an odd sort of half-wink, as if to confirm some secret plans we had made.

Aunt Macy didn't have much to say. She always got a little quiet around strangers. Then, too, she was the one who held the biggest grudge against Uncle Eugene, and I figured she was working out her own prejudices.

Papa leaned back in his chair and said, 'How's your father getting on, Norma?'

'Okay, I guess.'

'I haven't seen him in years.'

I noticed Aunt Macy tensing up. She started fiddling with her hair at the back of her neck, which was a nervous habit she had. I wanted to do something to make her relax but nothing came to mind. So I just sat still and picked at my meat loaf.

Bodean piped up suddenly, 'Do you know how to play spit 'n' cuss?'

Norma looked at him. 'What's that?'

'A card game,' I answered.

'No, I never heard of it. But I'd be happy to learn.'

Flood said, 'That boy'll worry you to death if you let him.'

Bodean started pouting, but Flood reached over and tousled his hair, which cheered him up a little. Flood isn't a real 'touchy' kind of person, and you have to take every gesture like that seriously. We all noticed it and smiled.

In that moment I felt good about my family. Everybody at that table was missing someone – a wife, a husband, a mother – but I still felt as if we were complete.

Papa said, 'You'll probably want to call your folks tonight, just to let them know you got here all right.'

Norma's face went still.

Then she shrugged and said, 'I don't know. Maybe.'

'I think you should,' Papa said gently.

'I told them I probably wouldn't call till tomorrow.'

'Well, whatever,' Papa said, and he gave Aunt Macy a quick look, as though this was something they both under-stood. But I didn't. I couldn't imagine not wanting to call your own home.

Aunt Macy suddenly stood up and said, 'I've fixed a coconut pie.'

'Aw, hell,' said Bodean, 'I hate coconut.'

Flood popped him on the head. 'Watch that mouth.'

Bodean rubbed his temple and said, 'I'll take a little piece, anyhow.'

After supper Norma went straight up to bed. I wanted to go up with her, but I figured she wanted to be alone and I didn't want to make a pest of myself.

I went into the living room and started ironing Papa's shirts. That was what I did just about every night before I went to sleep. Somehow over the years that had become my own personal job. Nobody could iron his shirts but me.

In the summer he wore the same half a dozen shirts over and over. They were all made out of denim and by now were faded and thin. I was always buying him new ones, but he just stuck them away in a drawer and never wore them. One Christmas Flood gave Papa a shirt, and Papa never even took it out of the plastic. The next Christmas Flood went through his drawer, got it out, and gave it to him again. Papa never knew the difference.

While I was ironing, Aunt Macy came in with a big bowl of homemade peach ice cream. I couldn't help worrying about her. She always ate too much when she was nervous. Her 'nerves' were legendary in our house. She had attacks of them, the way some people had attacks of arthritis. Papa said Aunt Macy was a peacemaker. She felt she had to keep everything under control. Anytime something interrupted the normal order of things, that's when Aunt Macy's nerves came on.

'What do you think of Norma?' I asked.

She shook her head and said, 'She looks so much like Eugene it's downright scary.'

I went on ironing shirts, working my way carefully around the buttons and wondering just what Aunt Macy was thinking about all this. She was a private person and didn't usually talk much about herself. For example, she'd lived with us all these years, and I really didn't know much about her past. I knew she'd been married twice and both her husbands had died young. But as to exactly how they died or why she never had any children, that much was still a mystery.

'Do you still hate Uncle Eugene?' I asked.

She gave me a wide-eyed look and said, 'What in the world makes you say that?'

'I don't know. I just figured you did. On account of what he did to Grandpa and Daddy.'

She was quiet for a second, then said, 'Honey, you don't ever hate your own blood.'

'Why not?'

'You just don't, that's all.'

'Well, it seems to me if people do bad things, you have to hate them whether they're related to you or not.'

'Oh, honey, it's not that easy,' she said. 'You know what they say, blood's thicker than water.'

'I know they say that. But I don't know what it means.'

Aunt Macy thought for a moment, then said, 'I was real disappointed in Eugene for a while. You come to expect things from your kin. Sometimes they let you down, but you never hate them.'

'Well, why did you stop speaking to him?'

When I looked at her I could tell that last question might have been pushing my luck a little.

'I don't know,' she said in a quiet voice. 'I guess I didn't really want to talk to him. Didn't have anything to say to him that he'd want to hear. After a while it was just a habit.'

She paused and took a tiny bite of ice cream. 'But that don't mean I hate him.'

I shot a spray of steam out of the iron and said, 'Do you think Flood hates Becky?'

'Well, now, that's different. Husbands and wives can hate each other real easy. It's the other side of love. When you get a little older you'll understand.'

The list of things I would know when I was older was steadily growing. I worried that her prediction wouldn't come true and that I would just go on being ignorant. How did it work . . . did someone just hand you a book when you turned the right age, full of the answers to all the questions you'd ever asked? The whole business left me flustered, and I let myself say something I probably shouldn't have.

'Did you ever hate your husbands?'

Aunt Macy dropped her spoon in the bowl with a clink.

'Lord, no,' she said. 'I married the two sweetest men in the world. I reckon they were so good that the Lord decided he couldn't do without them.'

She smiled as if she were remembering something. 'Well, that's not altogether true. I only remember the good things about them. That's one thing dying will do for you; it'll make people forget what was bad about you.'

I stood the iron on its end and turned it off. Aunt Macy was staring at the blank TV screen as if she thought there was a picture there.

'Like Mama?' I asked. All I'd ever heard were good things about her. I wondered if everyone had forgotten the bad.

The mention of Mama made Aunt Macy smile.

'Well, she was about as good as they come. Sweet and funny. She always made me laugh. She took charge of things. Seemed like nothing could go wrong as long as Judy was around.'

I smiled. I never thought of her as Judy. But the name sounded like someone everybody would like.

Aunt Macy sighed and said, 'I wish she could have lived to see you. I know she would have been proud. But Flood . . . well, there's times when I'm glad she isn't around to see that. There's times when he doesn't even seem like her son.'

'Flood's all right.'

'Used to be,' she said, 'but something's got into him lately.'

Suddenly I was tired from talking and just wanted to go to bed.

'Good night,' I said, giving Aunt Macy a kiss on the cheek.

'I'm sure it'll be all right.'

I didn't know what she meant by that. Probably some-thing to do with Flood.

When I came into my room, Norma was sitting on her bed writing in a little book. She had her hair pulled back in a braid, and her skin looked scrubbed and pink. She wore a big T-shirt that said, 'Hard Rock Cafe, New York.'

'Hi,' I said, feeling like I was intruding, even though it was my room.

She held up a finger until she finished writing a sentence and put a period at the end. Then she snapped her book shut and said, 'Done.'

'What is that?'

'A journal.'

'Like a diary?'

'Something like that. It's a strain sometimes, but it's necessary.'

'Why?'

'Because someday I plan to do something important enough that people will want to know about my history.'

'Oh,' I said.

'Don't you keep a journal?'

'Not really.'

'You should. You really ought to treat your life as if it's important because one day it might be.'

I already felt like my life was important, but I couldn't imagine anybody wanting to read about it.

'Do you write about your boyfriend?'

'Marshall? Yeah, some. But mostly I just write about my inner feelings.'

I nodded, wondering if I had any inner feelings.

'Do you miss him?' I asked. I couldn't help it. I was fascinated.

She leaned back, putting her hands behind her head. 'I don't let myself miss people.'

'Why not?'

'Because that's like needing them. I definitely don't need anybody.' She rolled over on her side, facing me. 'I'm on a solo mission. That's what Daddy says about me. "Don't worry about Norma. She's on a solo mission in life."'

She laughed and I did, too, just because it sounded funny.

'Is it always this quiet?' she asked.

'What do you mean?'

'There's no *noise* here.'

'Oh. Well, sometimes Flood makes noise when he comes in late.'

She didn't say anything to that. She just sat there looking at me, making me feel a little self-conscious. I undressed with my back turned, pulling my nightgown quickly over my head. I wished I had a T-shirt like hers. It had never occurred to me to sleep in anything but a nightgown.

'I like your room,' she said.

My heart swelled with pride, but I just shrugged. 'It's all right. Kinda plain, I guess.'

'But that's what I like. Everything is so basic. There's no clutter.' She paused and added, 'Except for those pictures.

Don't you hate it when your parents put dumb stuff like that in your room?'

All the pride I felt just evaporated. The pictures were the ones I had bought at the dime store. They were the only things in the room that really belonged to me. And they were the only things she didn't like.

'Oh, those,' I said, trying to laugh. 'I don't know where they came from.'

'Well, good night.'

I switched off the light and lay there in the darkness feeling young and stupid. Then Norma said, 'It's good having a cousin. Kind of like having a sister.'

And all my worries just flew away, like dried leaves in a strong wind.

Six

The next morning I got up early and slipped downstairs, being careful not to wake Norma up. She was sleeping soundly on her back, one hand dangling daintily over the bed. She looked as if she even knew how to sleep better than most people.

I started my chores, hoping to get them done so I could spend the day with Norma. Bodean was already up, and to my surprise he helped me scrub the kitchen without grumbling. From the window I could see the men working in the tobacco field. Even from a distance I could see that the crop didn't look right. By now it was usually ready for topping. That's when the leaves shoot up real fast and grow these big white blooms on the top and you have to pick them off so it can keep on growing.

The men in the field weren't topping, though. They were just standing around looking at the crop and shaking their heads. Watching them, I remembered the days when I used to help out. Papa didn't like me working in tobacco. He said the work was too hard for somebody my age. But when they were shorthanded I'd pitch in with everybody else.

It wasn't so bad at first, in the morning, when it was just

getting light. You'd kind of feel your way along the leaves and talk to whoever was around you. Lots of times somebody would start a song, and if you knew the words you could join in. By the time you stopped for breakfast you felt as if you had worked a whole day.

When the sun finally came up, it got pretty miserable. Your clothes would be drenched, your hair would be sticking to your forehead, and the gnats and flies would be buzzing around your face. Also the tobacco gum would start piling up on your fingers until your hands would get heavy. I always had to quit around lunchtime, but the others kept working right through the afternoon. When I thought about the bad parts, I was glad Papa never made me work if I didn't want to.

I always measured the summer by how the tobacco was doing. By the time the top leaves were being pulled, it was nearly time for school to start. I thought of it as a calendar, and without it I felt confused. Everything was thrown off balance.

Suddenly Bodean said, 'She ain't bad for a girl, is she?'

It startled me a little. I'd almost forgotten he was there.

'You mean Norma?'

He nodded, not looking at me.

'You like her, don't you?'

'Do me a favor.'

'Yes, sir,' I went on. 'I think Bodean's found himself a girlfriend.'

'Make me an offer,' he said, throwing a sponge at me.

'It's nothing to be ashamed of, Bodean. She's a pretty girl, and you're a handsome young man.'

'I'm gonna beat you up.'

'Why don't you ask her out on a date?'

That did it. He flew at me and started pounding me with his fists. His face was beet red, and there were angry tears in his eyes. I grabbed his wrists to make him stop beating me.

'What's got into you?' I asked.

'I hate you,' he said, wiping at his eyes. 'I wish she lived here instead of you.'

'Oh, really? Well, maybe she'll stay here and I'll go off to the city to live.'

'I wish you would.'

'Go on now and sweep off the back porch.'

'No.'

'Don't give me trouble today, Bodean. I'm not in the mood for it.'

He pouted and gave me a kick in the shins for good measure. Then he went off to the back porch, with no intention of sweeping it. Instead, I heard the door slam, and a few seconds later I saw him running across the yard toward the field. He was probably going to tell Flood on me, but that didn't concern me too much.

Around ten o'clock Norma came down. By then I had cleaned the whole downstairs and helped Aunt Macy with two loads of laundry. Aunt Macy kept looking at her watch and saying, 'She sure likes to sleep late, doesn't she?' Everything in the house revolved around Norma now. I

43

wondered how we ever got along without her.

She came down wearing a midriff and a pair of cutoff denims. Her hair was thick and a little wrinkled from having been in a braid all night. She wore a tiny little gold chain around her left ankle. Next to her I felt sloppy, even though I had put on my best shorts and a clean white blouse.

'Morning, everybody,' she said, coming into the kitchen. 'I overslept a little.'

Aunt Macy said, 'I reckon so. You got worn out from that long trip. Let me get you some breakfast.'

She fixed us pancakes and allowed us both a cup of coffee. Norma drank hers like it was nothing special.

'What do you feel like doing?' I asked.

'Anything's fine with me.'

'It's too hot to ride bikes. We could go over to Blue Hole.'

She wrinkled up her nose and laughed. 'What's that? It sounds scary.'

'It's just a swimming place. It's this part of Blue Stone Creek where the water gets real deep.'

'Like a lake?'

'Sort of, only not that big. It's in the woods. There are all these big rocks to jump off of.' The more I described it, the sillier it sounded. I hadn't spent a whole lot of time thinking about Blue Hole. I'd gone swimming there for as long as I could remember. There were lots of places on the creek where you could go, but Blue Hole was the best. It was kind of secluded and the water was deep enough to dive into. You could sunbathe on the banks or wander up the path until the creek turned quick and bubbly again. I couldn't imagine her not liking it.

'Are there snakes?' she asked.

'No, not really. About once a year somebody sees one, but the boys always kill it with a rock or something.'

'Boys?'

'Yeah.'

'What kind?'

'You know. Regular boys.'

She nodded, biting on her top lip. After a while she said, 'Why not? I've never been swimming in a creek before.'

Norma went upstairs to change. I already had my bathing suit on under my clothes, so I just stood by the door waiting for her. When she came down, she was wearing a large black T-shirt that hit her at the top of her legs and a pair of sandals. Her hair was back in a braid. She was flawless. She was the kind of person who made you want to run to the mirror to see if you had something stuck between your front teeth.

As we were getting ready to leave, Bodean came wandering in.

'Where you going, ugly?' he asked.

Norma said, 'Is that any way to talk to your long lost cousin?'

He turned red and answered without looking at her. 'I won't talking to you. I was talking to her.'

He gave me a kick in the shin.

'Well, is that any way to talk to your aunt?'

45

'She ain't my aunt.'

'She's your father's sister, isn't she?'

'She might be his sister, but she ain't my aunt.'

I didn't even try to argue with him. He was in one of those moods.

'Well, she's my cousin and she's not ugly. So you better apologize or you can't go swimming with us.'

'Maybe I don't want to go,' he said, though he did, worse than anything.

'Fine. We'll go without you.'

She opened the door, and Bodean ran around in front of us.

He said, 'I'm sorry I called you ugly, ugly.'

'That's close enough,' said Norma, and he followed along behind us as we walked toward Blue Hole, chucking rocks at the squirrels as they ran across the power lines.

We walked through the woods, trying to steer clear of the poison ivy. Bodean had learned to identify it in Cub Scouts, so now we couldn't walk past a single leaf without him screaming.

'You're just a regular pioneer,' Norma said about the fifth time he pushed her away.

'I know what mushrooms are poisonous, too,' he assured her.

The path to Blue Hole was well worn by now, and even before the water was visible you could hear the voices and splashes of the swimmers.

'I love this,' Norma said. 'It's all so . . . natural.'

'Where do you go swimming in Richmond?'

'In the pool.'

'You have a pool?'

'Oh, no,' she said, laughing. 'We belong to a club.'

'Oh,' I said, feeling stupid, but then Blue Hole came into sight and I got too excited to worry.

It was already crowded. The big rock was full of people, jumping and diving and horsing around. The smaller rocks had girls sunbathing on them. And the banks were crowded with mothers and children. The rocks were strictly for the kids my age. There was a definite code of order, and everybody knew where they belonged.

I was glad that as Norma saw Blue Hole, it looked its best. The sun was shining down from a cloudless sky, making the water bluer than it really was, and all the trees around it looked green and fresh.

I was so caught up in the sight that I almost didn't notice Kenny and Ethan sitting up on the big rock, their heads turned hard in our direction.

Bodean said, 'I'm gonna do a backflip off that rock.'

'Come on,' I said to Norma, and she followed as we made our way to the rock. Kenny and Ethan kept staring as we climbed up to where they were sitting.

Kenny ran his fingers through his wet hair and crossed his arms, trying to make his muscles look bigger.

'If it ain't Dutch Peyton,' Kenny said, but he was looking at Norma.

'Kenny and Ethan, this is my cousin, Norma.'

They nodded at her. She just smiled. They mumbled something about the water being cold.

Then Norma proceeded to take off her T-shirt. She was wearing a red bikini that only covered the essentials. She had perfect breasts and a flat stomach. Even though her legs were pale, they curved in all the right spots and were full of muscles, like an athlete's. Aunt Macy said men didn't like women with muscular legs, but obviously she was wrong. Kenny and Ethan both looked like a strong wind could have knocked them over.

'It sure is hot,' Norma said.

I took off my shorts but left my T-shirt on. I wasn't ready to expose myself yet. Norma spread her towel and sat down. The thing that amazed me the most was how she didn't even seem to be aware of this perfect body she lived in.

'Look, Norma,' Bodean said, and he did a backwards cannonball into the water.

'He's cute.' Norma chuckled.

Kenny and Ethan moved over beside her, still gaping.

Finally Kenny said, 'What do you think of Marston?'

'I haven't seen much of it,' she said. 'It seems nice.'

'It's kind of boring,' Ethan said. 'You'll figure that out pretty soon.'

'It'll be nice to be bored,' she said, and her voice sounded sad. Then it changed, and she started asking them questions about themselves. I took that opportunity to remove my T-shirt. As long as she was talking I knew they wouldn't look at me.

I sat there hugging my knees to my chest and looking out at the water. The Grogan boys were splashing around in the shallow part, cigarettes dangling from their lips. Charlene Crab and Marcia Meadows were sitting nearby. They were the most popular girls at school, and they looked a little put out at having lost Kenny's and Ethan's attention. In fact, almost everybody was looking at Norma, even the grown women with children. It felt funny having all those eyes looking in my direction and none of them seeing me. I was starting to feel invisible.

I heard a squeal and looked over to see that the Grogan boys were splashing water in Bodean's face. He was swinging his fists at them and missing, and they were laughing and splashing even harder. I got to my feet in a flash.

'Hey, you just watch it!' I shouted. The Grogans looked up at me. 'You let that boy alone!'

'Aw, we ain't bothering him,' said Daryl Grogan, the oldest and the ugliest. Then he took his hand and pushed Bodean's head under the water. I jumped in and swam over there. The Grogans just looked at me, grinning around their cigarettes. I took Bodean by the shoulders and moved him away.

'You stupid old rednecks! Why don't you pick on somebody your own size?'

'You got somebody in mind?' Daryl asked.

'You want us to pick on you?' said Jimmy.

Next thing I knew Jimmy had grabbed me and slung me over his shoulder.

I started kicking and screaming, but he was as strong as he was dumb, and I couldn't get loose. Bodean flew at them, but Daryl grabbed him and threw him out in the water like a beach ball. Finally they dumped me on the grass. They dumped Bodean right beside me, and we sat there coughing and catching our breath. Charlene and Marcia were cackling like hens.

Kenny and Ethan had jumped in, as though they might have been trying to help us. But they were too late, and now they stood waist-deep in water, looking first at the Grogans and then at us.

'You okay?' Ethan yelled.

I just nodded, coughing up water. Norma looked serene and beautiful up on that rock, as tantalizing as a mermaid. And there I was, plopped on the ground like a sack of potatoes. All because of Bodean. He was ruining my life.

'Why can't you keep yourself out of trouble?' I snapped.

He spit some water on the grass and said, 'Shoot, I ain't scared of them.'

Seven

By the time we walked home, I was feeling bruised and battered and pretty humble. I didn't want to say anything. The scene at Blue Hole had the opposite effect on Bodean. He was making up for his humiliation by bragging about his talents. It was hot, and the sound of his voice was starting to exhaust both Norma and me.

'Last spring I shot me three grouse in one day. Do you know what a grouse is?'

'No, I don't,' Norma said with a weary smile.

'It's a little old bird. It ain't easy to shoot something that little. Some folks think it's a big deal to shoot a deer, but it's a lot harder to hit a teeny-weeny old bird. My daddy said I was the best grouse hunter he'd ever seen for my age.'

Norma sighed. 'Well, I just don't know why you'd want to shoot an innocent little bird that never did a thing to you.'

Bodean was stunned for a second. He'd never considered the ethical side of hunting. I never had myself since I grew up with it. I just thought everybody hunted. But now that Norma mentioned it, it did seem cruel.

Bodean fumbled for a bit, then came up with an answer.

'You shoot 'em so you can eat 'em. I mean, you eat chickens, don't you? And a chicken never did anything to you.'

I was impressed. I'd never heard Bodean talk that smart.

'Well, it seems to me,' Norma said, 'that there's enough meat in the supermarket without going out and killing more.'

Bodean gave her a hard look, then pouted at the ground. I was feeling confused. Norma had a way of saying things that made you want to believe them, even if you didn't agree.

Suddenly she turned to me and said, 'Would your daddy mind if I made a long-distance phone call?'

'No, go ahead. He said you ought to call your parents.'

'Oh, that. Well, I was really thinking of Marshall.'

'Don't you want to call your parents?'

She hesitated, then said, 'My parents and I don't communicate.'

'Oh,' I said as if I understood. She made it sound like no one with any sense communicated with their parents.

'Those guys were kind of nice,' she said, changing the subject. 'Are they good friends of yours?'

'Kenny and Ethan?'

'They've got a certain charm.'

I could think of a lot of words that applied to Kenny and Ethan, but I wasn't sure charm was one of them.

'I suppose.'

'Do you think we should go to their softball game tomorrow? I told them we would.'

'You did?'

'Yeah. I hope you don't mind. It sounded like fun.'

'No. I mean, yeah, it would be fun. They usually win.'

Bodean said, 'You eat steak, don't you? A cow never did nothing to you.'

'Bodean,' Norma said in a voice that wasn't quite so pleasant, 'I just don't want to talk about animals anymore if it's all the same to you.'

Bodean shrugged.

'Make me an offer,' he said blankly, as if he had lost faith in his saying. I looked at him, and he seemed so skinny and small. I remembered the way he looked when the Grogans were picking on him, this tiny little person alone in a mean world. Somewhere along the line I had stopped being mad at him and I wanted to protect him. It seemed like my job.

When we got back to the house, Papa was standing in the front yard talking to two men I'd never seen before. They were wearing suits, and that made them look odd. The men around here never dressed up except for church. Even from a distance I could see that Papa's face was drawn and worried. The two men were doing all the talking, and as we got closer, I could hear the dull rhythm of their voices but couldn't make out any words.

'Who's that?' Norma asked, shading her eyes.

'I don't know.'

'It looks serious.'

'Oh, it's probably just . . .' But I couldn't even come up with a guess.

'We probably shouldn't interrupt.'

'Let's go sit in the shade,' I said.

We went and sat down under the big hickory tree, though it really wasn't that much cooler in the shade. Bodean immediately started climbing the tree, showing off again, but Norma had long ago forgotten about him. And I was busy staring at those men. One of them was pointing his finger in Papa's face, but Papa was just looking at the ground, digging his work boot into the grass.

'Hey, y'all!' came a voice from above.

I looked up. Bodean was perched on a limb.

'Get down from there before you break your neck,' I snapped.

'Do me a favor.'

After a moment Flood came out of the house and walked up beside Papa. He took off his hat and wiped his brow. He was frowning even more than usual, more than he did when Papa bought the wrong tractor. If I were those men I would have been scared of him.

Norma said, 'Your brother is fascinating, isn't he?'

'What do you mean?'

'He's an enigma.'

'He is?'

'You know, like a puzzle.'

'Oh. I guess.'

'He seems so strong . . . and sad at the same time.'

She stared at him, chewing on the end of her braid. Finally she said, 'What happened with him and his wife?'

I looked up at Bodean. He was three limbs high and paying no attention to us.

'I don't know. She just left.'

'She had to have a reason. I mean, did he ask her to leave?'

'No. I don't think so. He doesn't really talk about it.'

'And why didn't she take Bodean with her?'

'I don't know,' I said, feeling irritable. 'I guess that's her business.'

'It seems like a selfish thing to do.'

'You don't even know her,' I said. 'You don't know the first thing about her.'

'That's why I'm asking,' she said coolly.

I looked away. Papa and Flood were shaking hands with the men now. That made me feel a little better. The men got into their car, a brand new Cadillac. Papa and Flood stood together, watching them. Then Flood turned and went back in the house, but Papa stood very still as the car drove off, leaving behind a cloud of dust.

'She probably just wasn't strong enough for him,' Norma said. 'A strong man needs a strong woman.'

I didn't have a chance to reply. Papa had seen us and was heading in our direction.

Bodean yelled, 'Y'all look at me!'

I did. He seemed much too far off the ground.

'Get down, Bodean! This instant!' I shouted.

'Girls are scared of everything,' he grumbled, starting to ease his way down the limbs.

'Hello, ladies,' Papa said. 'Y'all have a nice swim?'

55

'Very nice, thank you, Uncle Earl,' Norma said politely. It was strange to hear someone call him Uncle.

'What did those men want?' I asked.

'Oh, nothing,' he said with a sigh. 'They're just from the bank.'

'What bank?'

'The one that gave us the loan on the farm. Every year they like to come out and check up on us. Want to make sure they've made a good investment.'

'Why were they pointing at you like that?'

He sighed and shook his head. His hair had little bits of gray all through it that glistened in the sunlight like flecks of snow. I'd never noticed them before.

'I don't know, honey. I don't know why folks behave the way they do. But don't you worry about it.'

Bodean had made his way down, not without skinning both his knees.

'Grandpa, did you see me up there?'

'Uh-huh.'

'I was way up high.'

'You sure were,' he said.

Then as he turned away, he mumbled something, as though he was talking to himself. But I heard him.

He said, 'Anybody can climb high, long as they've got something to step on.'

With that he started walking toward the house. We followed without asking questions. Suddenly the whole day felt like a tire with a slow leak.

Eight

After supper Flood went into town, and the rest of us sat out in the front yard eating watermelon. It wasn't as hot as it had been, but the air was sticky and humid. The moon was already out even though it was still light, and the sky was a pale blue.

'The devil's beating his wife,' Bodean said.

'What?' Norma asked.

'When the moon comes out before it gets dark . . . it means the devil's beating his wife,' I explained.

She laughed. 'What in the world makes you think the devil has a wife?'

I shrugged. 'It's just a saying.'

When we finished our watermelon, Norma taught me how to do cartwheels and handstands. She was on the gymnastics team at her school and knew all kinds of stunts. I caught on pretty fast, and Norma said I'd be a good gymnast myself.

'We don't have that at my school,' I said.

'You don't? Well, maybe you could be a cheer-leader.'

'Maybe,' I said, but I didn't know how to tell her that only girls like Charlene Crab and Marcia Meadows could be cheerleaders, girls with long legs and bubbly laughs and hair that swished when they walked. The only club I belonged to was Future Homemakers of America.

Papa and Aunt Macy sat in rocking chairs on the front porch, talking in quiet voices. I wanted to hear what they were saying; it sounded like worried talk. I tried to stay near the porch, but Norma kept distracting me with some new stunt. She could balance on her hands for ages, her back slightly arched, her arms not even trembling from the weight. Bodean pretended not to be impressed.

'Aw, that ain't nothing,' he said. He proceeded to stand on his head for a half a second before falling over hard on his behind.

'Where do you think Flood went?' Norma asked as we sat down again, exhausted from all our jumping around.

'Probably playing pool,' I said. He usually did that only on weekends, but he'd been going out a lot more often lately.

'Oh,' Norma said, resting her chin on her knees. 'How old did you say he was?'

I hadn't said how old he was. In fact, I wasn't even sure. 'I reckon he's about thirty-two. He was just out of high school when I was born.'

'Does he have a girlfriend?'

'Of course not. He's married.'

'You mean they're not divorced by now?'

'Oh. Well, technically he's divorced. But Becky's still his wife. I mean, she's still Bodean's mother.' I wasn't sure what

58

I meant. I didn't like to think of Flood and Becky as being divorced. That meant Becky didn't have a connection to us anymore, except to Bodean, and even that didn't seem too strong.

'Don't you think it's about time he got on with his life?' Norma asked.

'His life is fine.'

'Well, it seems to me something's missing.'

Bodean came forward then, holding his hands out in front of him, cupped together like he was carrying water.

'Got something for you,' he said to Norma.

'What is it?'

'Just something.'

Norma blinked at him, then extended her palm with a sigh. Bodean uncupped his hands, and a lightningbug flew out, its tail glowing a fiery orange. Norma let out a little scream and swatted at it. Bodean giggled.

'You little brat!' she shouted. 'Somebody ought to give you a good spanking!'

Bodean looked as if she'd just slapped him in the face. Slowly his bottom lip started to protrude. That was his crying face. I'd seen it many times before.

'Somebody ought to spank you, too!' he yelled and took off running in the other direction.

'Why'd you do that?' I asked. 'He was only giving you a present.'

'I don't want a present. I just want to be left alone.'

She looked away from me then, staring out at the empty

road that ran past our house. I waited for her to apologize, but she didn't seem in any hurry to do that.

So I said, 'Don't you like it here?'

She looked at me as if I'd said something outrageous.

'Oh, sure,' she answered. 'I just love being sent off to a house full of people I don't even know.'

'Well, maybe you should leave,' I said. I couldn't believe we were having a fight. Just when we seemed to be getting along so well.

'Where would I go?'

'Home.'

'Right,' she said.

She stood up and brushed off the seat of her shorts. Then she walked toward the house, and a wave of fear passed over me, as if she really was going to go pack her bags.

She walked right past Papa and Aunt Macy without a word and slammed the door behind her. Papa looked at me like it was something I did. I stared down at my toes, which were green with grass stain. I felt miserable.

After a few minutes I got up and went after Norma.

Papa said, 'What's up?' when I passed him, but I just shrugged.

I found Norma sitting on the floor of my bedroom in a full split. She was leaning over, holding her foot in both hands and touching her forehead to her knee. It was hard to believe anybody could do that with their body. It looked like she might be hurting herself.

'Hi,' she said without looking up.

'Hi.'

Finally she raised up and smiled at me. 'I have to do my exercises so I can stay limber.'

I stared at her. She seemed to have forgotten everything.

'I guess I'm sorry,' I said, though I really wanted her to say it first.

'Sorry for what?'

'For our fight.'

'We didn't have a fight.'

'Well, what was that just then?'

She thought for a second and then laughed. 'That was just me being moody and horrible. I should have warned you. I have terrible moods. I just kind of snap sometimes, but it doesn't mean I'm mad. Did you think I was mad?'

'Well, yeah. I did.'

'You're pretty sensitive, aren't you?' she asked, bending over her other leg and staying that way for a long time. When she came back up again, her face was pink from where the blood had rushed to it.

'I guess maybe I am,' I said, though I hadn't really thought about it before.

'That's a good quality to have.' She crossed her legs Indian-style and studied me for a moment. 'Men like sensitive women. Marshall says I'm not sensitive enough, and I guess he's right about that. That's the thing I like about Marshall. He's got me figured out.'

I sat down next to her, wondering how long it would take me to figure her out. She kept my head in a spin, the way she changed so quickly. Feelings just seemed to pass through her, like water through a bottomless glass.

'Do you and Marshall fight a lot?' I asked.

'You use that word too much,' she said. 'Maybe that's because you've never really seen a fight.'

'Yes, I have.'

She shook her head. 'Your family bickers some. They argue, maybe. But a fight's something else altogether. It goes down deep. It makes you feel like your insides are being ripped out. You've never seen anything like that, have you?'

I just stared at her. Her voice was scaring me. She hugged her knees to her chest and leaned her chin on them.

'No, Marshall and I don't fight. We clash occasionally.'

'Well, what do you clash about?'

'Little things. Like football, for example. He's obsessed with it. I say it's just an excuse to hit people, and he says I don't understand it. Men are entirely too caught up in sports, anyway. Don't you agree?'

'Yeah, I guess. Ethan's that way. He'd rather hit a softball than eat when he's hungry.'

She nodded and bit her bottom lip. 'I thought so.'

'What?'

'You like him, don't you?'

I stiffened. 'No . . . I mean, just as a friend.'

'Come on, Dutch. It's all over your face when you look at him.'

'It is?'

'He must know it. Or maybe he doesn't. Guys are kind of slow that way.'

'I don't have a crush on Ethan,' I said. 'At least, I don't think I do.'

'Oh, come on. We're friends, aren't we? You don't have to keep secrets from me.'

It seemed impossible to keep secrets from her, even if I wanted to. She knew things about me before I knew them myself. So that was why my hands got all clammy around Ethan; that was why my heart jumped and sputtered when I saw him. I figured it was just nerves, like Aunt Macy.

'Don't tell anyone,' I said in a near whisper. 'Please.'

'Who would I tell?'

'I don't know. But I'd just die . . . I'd kill myself if anyone found out.'

'Oh, you would not. Don't be so dramatic.'

'Well, I didn't mean that.'

'Look, if you're trying to get him interested you're going about it all wrong. You can't go around wearing your feelings on your face.'

'I didn't know I was.'

'That's why I'm telling you. You can't put yourself on the line like that. Once the secret's out, you lose your advantage.'

'What should I do?' I hated how desperate my voice sounded. I felt exposed now that I had admitted to this crush. It was scary to let a feeling like that loose in the world.

'Well, first of all, when you get around him you should

ignore him for a while. Let him get worried. Do all your flirting with the other one.'

'Kenny?'

She nodded. 'That'll make him jealous. And once he gets jealous, it's all downhill from there.'

'You do this a lot?'

'All the time. It's something I happen to believe in. Indifference is your only protection.'

'Protection from what?'

'Everything. And everybody. Keep yourself closed. Make them wonder.'

'How did you learn all this?' I asked.

She shrugged. 'Experience.'

She leaned back on her elbows, shaking her hair behind her. 'It works on everything, not just guys. You can protect yourself from anything if you know how. When something's bothering you, just look past it and say, "I don't care." Try it sometime.'

I thought about the tobacco drying up under the harsh afternoon sun. I said to myself, 'I don't care.' But it just sounded foolish and hollow, like any other lie.

'Don't worry, we'll get him interested,' she said, as if making her own private plans. I wanted to hear more of her strategy, but before I could ask, Bodean appeared in the doorway.

He stood there, looking at his feet and pretending not to notice us.

'What do you want?' I asked.

'Nothing. I just wanted y'all to know I'm not speaking to you no more.'

'Is that so?'

He nodded. 'So don't try talking to me cause I ain't talking back.'

Norma said, 'Well, I'm real sorry to hear that. I was hoping we could be friends again.'

'Do me a favor,' he said, looking up at her.

'And you're right, somebody does need to give me a spanking. Somebody needs to take a switch to my legs.'

He grinned.

'You're too big for a spanking.'

'Can you forgive me?'

Bodean struggled to hide his excitement. Finally he just shrugged and said, 'I'll let you know.'

'Oh, come on. I know you like me, even if you are mad.'

'I don't like you too much,' he said. Then, 'Maybe a little.'

'That's better.' She got up and walked toward him. He watched her with big eyes. 'Now how about a kiss?'

He backed away and said, 'I ain't kissing no girl!'

And with that he turned and darted off down the stairs. Norma looked at me, and we burst into giggles.

'God, I love to tease him,' she said. 'I just can't resist it.'

I smiled in agreement, but I wished her voice had sounded a little warmer when she said it.

Nine

That night before I went to bed, I started a journal. I used an old notebook left over from school. Norma said that would do until I could get something better. She told me I should start by putting the date at the top, and then I should just write down whatever feelings came to mind.

'Like what?' I asked.

'Anything.'

I waited. Nothing came to mind.

'How does yours start?' I asked.

'It's kind of personal.'

'Oh.'

She hesitated. 'Well, I guess I can read you a little bit.' She cleared her throat. ' "A warm summer night. Outside the crickets are talking back and forth. They seem to be speaking to me. They sound lost and alone." '

'That's beautiful,' I said.

She shrugged and continued. ' "It was an eventful day. Dutch and I went swimming at a place called Blue Hole. There we met two boys named Kenny and Ethan. They were the sweet and humble type, the kind you might find between the pages of a charming little book." '

'They are?'

'Well, you have to embellish. You can't just say I met two boys and leave it at that. You have to describe. That's the essence of writing.'

'Oh.'

'The thing is, you have to plan on someone reading your journal one day. Not any time soon, but long after you're famous or even dead. You want to make your life sound as good as possible.'

'Okay,' I said doubtfully. It seemed a little bit like lying.

She continued. ' "Kenny was handsome in a ruffian sort of way. I found him the more attractive of the two, but Dutch favors the other one, Ethan." '

'Hold on,' I said, getting nervous. 'That's a secret.'

Norma frowned. 'You're supposed to put secrets in your journal. That's what it's for.'

'But what if somebody finds it?' I was thinking of Bodean.

'That's the chance you're taking with a journal. It's part of the thrill.'

'Well, just make sure you hide it good,' I said. 'Go ahead.'

'Well, then it *really* gets personal. But that's pretty much how it should go.'

I said okay, and she went back to writing. Her pen moved quickly, and her tongue slid across her lip as she wrote. I looked back at my blank pages.

Finally I wrote: 'Today Norma and I went swimming at Blue Hole, and Kenny and Ethan were there. I think Norma has a crush on Kenny, but maybe I'm just imagining it.'

I stopped, rereading the lines. It didn't sound as pretty as Norma's, but at least it was a start. I chewed on my pen for a second, then started again: 'Me and Bodean got in a fight with the Grogan boys. It was real embarrassing. I just felt like the biggest fool on earth. All because of Bodean. Sometimes I think that boy is going to ruin my life.'

I stopped and scratched that out. I was thinking of how upset Bodean would get if he ever found it and read it. I didn't care what Norma said about taking chances. It didn't seem right to hurt someone's feelings if you really cared about them.

Then I wrote, 'Two men were talking to Papa when we got back home. They looked mad. It had me worried, but Papa said . . .'

I stopped. I was losing interest. What was the point of writing down your life? It was enough trouble just trying to live it.

Norma noticed I had stopped, and she looked over at me.

'What's wrong?'

'I'm not enjoying this.'

'Why not?'

'It's like watching a rerun. I already know what's gonna happen.'

'But that's the good part — you can make it a little different. You can rearrange the truth.'

'Maybe tomorrow,' I said, and I put the notebook away.

Norma finished writing, and I turned off the light. I

thought we might talk a little, but after a second I heard her breathing deep and steady, and I knew she was asleep. My mind was buzzing with thoughts. I wondered what would happen when I saw Ethan, if Norma's advice might work. The longer I thought, the harder it was to sleep. Eventually I just got tired of tossing and turning, and my stomach was starting to rumble. I decided to go downstairs and get a piece of lemon pound cake.

As I was tiptoeing downstairs I saw a light on in the kitchen. Then I heard low voices. It was Papa and Flood. I couldn't hear the words they were saying, but I desperately wanted to. Eavesdropping is a terrible habit of mine. It seems to be the only way to find out anything interesting.

I sat down on the bottom step and peeked around the door. From there I could see them as long as they stayed at the table, and I could hear their voices pretty well.

Flood was talking the most and the loudest.

'I'm just saying get out while we can. Why stick around and wait for them to start hauling our equipment away?'

'I don't believe in giving up,' Papa said quietly. 'I'm not a quitter.'

'You always were the stubbornest man that ever drew a breath. What do you think you're gonna solve by sticking around here? You think some angel of the Lord is gonna come down from the sky and save this crop? Even if we make money on this one . . . which we won't . . . we're gonna be in debt up to our eyeballs.'

Papa said, 'A man has his pride to consider.'

70

'Pride hell. What good's your pride gonna do when they come and take that tractor away? Not that it would be any great loss, that piece of junk. If you ask me, that's where all the trouble started.'

'I don't recall asking you,' Papa said, his voice getting louder.

'That's the problem, isn't it? You don't ask me about anything. You don't care what I think. It's your way or nothing.'

'I know what you think. Everything that's gone wrong is my fault. But I can't help the state of the economy. And I sure as hell can't help the weather.'

'I told you not to take out all those loans in the first place.'

'If we hadn't, we would have lost the farm.'

'We're gonna lose it anyway, aren't we?'

'Not if I can help it.'

'Well, it's like you said. You can't help it.'

Papa pounded his fist on the table. The sound of it boomed off the walls.

'Now, you listen to me. I've had about enough of your mouth. If you spent half as much energy working as you do complaining, maybe we wouldn't be in this fix.'

'Oh, that's right. Blame it on me.'

'I'm not blaming anybody. But I know this. We got through hard times before. My father and Eugene and I worked this farm by ourselves, and we never took a loss. Eugene used to do the work of ten men. Eugene . . .'

'Eugene isn't here anymore! I am!'

When their voices stopped, the whole house got as silent as a graveyard. They sat very still at the table, looking away from each other.

'You want too much from me,' Flood finally said. 'I told you I wasn't a farmer. I told you I wasn't any good at this. You're the one that made me stay.'

'I never made you.'

Flood laughed, a bitter laugh. 'I know what happens to anybody who tries to leave here. I know what you think of that.'

'I don't blame Eugene for leaving,' Papa said. 'I blame him for ignoring his obligation.'

'And what obligation is that?'

'To his family.'

'Oh, yes, the almighty family. That's all you care about, isn't it? You're so busy trying to pull everybody together. But if you really cared about this family, you'd let us go.'

Papa said, 'One day you're gonna learn you can't turn your back on things.'

'The way you turned your back on Eugene?'

'That's my business, not yours.'

'You're something else. You've got a whole set of rules for everybody, and a whole different set for yourself. You don't walk it like you talk it.'

'At least I've got rules. I know the importance of them.'

'Yes, sir, you worship them. Long as you're the one making them.'

They were quiet for a long time. Flood stood up and

went to the door. Then Papa said, 'I feel like I don't even know you anymore.'

'Maybe you never did,' said Flood. 'Ever think about that?'

'Yes. I think about it.' Then, after a moment he added, 'You're free to do as you please.'

'I'm free,' Flood huffed. 'I'm about as free as one of those cows out there. I can move around long as I stay inside your fences.'

Flood opened the back door, and Papa said, 'That's right. Run away. That's your answer to everything.'

'If it was, I'd have been gone a long time ago.'

And with that he walked out and slammed the door.

Papa sat real still at the table, rubbing his forehead with a big, callused hand. He let out a deep, slow sigh. It looked as if he might get up, but he didn't. He just shifted his weight and started rubbing his head again.

I got up some courage and walked into the kitchen. He didn't hear me, and I had to clear my throat to make him notice. He raised his eyes to me and smiled.

'Dutch,' he said, 'What are you doing up so late?'

'Couldn't sleep.'

'Did you hear us talking?'

'Just a little.'

He stretched his arms out to me, and I went over and sat in his lap. I didn't fit there as well as I used to, but his arms still felt strong around me.

'We're going through some hard times,' he said. 'But

we'll get through them okay. We always have before.' He paused, then said, 'When your mama died, I didn't think we'd ever bounce back. But we did, and life went on, and we're still a family. That's the important thing. Families are important, Dutch. They're about the only thing you can count on. Do you understand?'

'I reckon.'

'The world's a big place, and it'll call out to you, but you can't get away from your roots, no matter how far you go.'

He wasn't making much sense anymore, and it worried me, so I changed the subject.

'Are we gonna lose the farm?'

'No,' he said firmly.

'How do you know?'

'Because I have faith. That's something your brother doesn't understand.'

'Flood's not a bad person, is he?'

Papa shook his head. 'He's not bad. He's just real confused right now. He's got a lot of anger inside of him, and he's got to learn to let that go.'

'Anger at you?'

'At me. And at Becky. At the whole world, really. Some folks start seeing how things might have been, and they can't see nothing else.'

'How'd he get like that?'

'I don't know, child,' Papa said. 'I wish I did.'

Ten

Norma and I spent a long time getting ready for the softball game the next day, and most of the preparations centered around me.

'You have the potential to be a knockout,' Norma told me. 'You've got good facial features. All we need to do is bring them out.'

The first step was to put my hair in a French braid. Norma said it was at a boring length; it fell in a square cut around my shoulders. She also said that it was an unfortunate color. A little bit mousy, she called it.

'We'll just tuck it away till you can get some highlights in it.'

After that she did something to my face she called 'contouring.' That was supposed to make my cheek-bones more defined.

But when I looked in the mirror I didn't see a new woman; I just saw me with a lot of makeup on. My face was still too round, my nose was still pugged, my freckles still peeked through the thick coat of foundation.

'You look like a whore,' Bodean said.

'You don't even know what a whore is,' I said, kicking at him.

'Yes, I do. It's a lady who don't go to church.'

Norma and I giggled.

'Where'd you hear that from?' she asked.

'I heard Daddy say it once. He said Aunt Macy was as nervous as a whore in church.'

Norma giggled again, but I was annoyed. I couldn't believe the things Flood said around that child.

'You shouldn't believe everything your daddy says.'

'Why not?'

'Because he's not God.'

'I know he ain't God,' Bodean said, rolling his eyes but looking like he wasn't too sure about that at all.

'Well, I think you look great,' Norma said, 'and Ethan's a fool if he doesn't think so, too.'

'Norma!' I hissed.

But it was too late. Bodean's ears were even faster than his mouth.

'Ethan who?'

'Nobody. We better get going.' I was trying hard not to be furious at Norma.

'You mean that old red-haired boy, Ethan Cole?' Bodean said. 'Is he your sweetheart?'

'No, he's not. Now go on before I slap you.'

'Dutch has got a sweetheart, Dutch has got a sweetheart,' he chanted. 'And he's *ugly!*'

I raised my hand with every intention of swatting him, but he just giggled and ran out of the room. Norma was smiling with her hand over her mouth.

'You think that's funny?' I challenged her.

'Oh, he's just a little boy.'

'A little boy with a big mouth.'

'You worry too much.'

'I don't care. You can't go around telling people's secrets like that. That was private information.' Turning back toward the mirror, I felt a lump rise in my throat. 'And on top of everything, I look like a fool!'

'You do not. You look fine.'

I took my hair out of the braid and shook it loose. While I was doing that, I caught sight of Norma in the mirror. She had this wounded look on her face, and I suddenly felt bad.

'After I did all that work,' she said.

'I just didn't like it,' I said weakly. 'It looks fine on you but not on me.'

'At least leave the makeup,' she said. It seemed real important to her so I gave in.

'All right. But please don't tell anyone else about Ethan.'

'I said I was sorry.'

I didn't say anything to that. She *hadn't* said she was sorry. But I felt she probably was, in her own way.

We didn't talk much during the walk to the ball park. The boys played their games at the church softball field, which was about half a mile away from my house if you cut through the woods. Norma wasn't very comfortable in the woods. She took slow, careful steps and jumped every time there was a sound.

'There's nothing to be scared of,' I told her.

'Who's scared?' was her answer.

The first inning had started by the time we got there. There was just a small crowd sitting in lawn chairs – mostly parents, drinking lemonade and fanning themselves and talking about the weather. We sat on the ground, making clover chains and sipping on Cokes, looking up every now and then to see how close the game was to being over.

'Do you think you will marry Marshall?' I asked Norma. I had let the subject drop for a while, but I was still curious.

'I don't think I'm going to marry anybody. Marriage is an unnatural state.'

'It is?'

She nodded. 'All that garbage about for better or worse, sickness and health, blah, blah, blah. Who are they kidding? Like anybody knows what they're going to do ten years from now.'

'But everybody gets married. It's a commitment.'

'I don't believe in commitments.'

'Well, what about love?'

She leaned back on her elbows, looking at the sky.

'Love is a series of short spasms. Somebody famous said that. A poet, I think.'

'Well, he probably never met the right woman.'

She laughed, staring up at the clouds. 'You're so funny, Dutch.'

I hadn't meant to be funny. I said, 'Well, I think being married is better than being alone.'

She looked at me. 'What do you know about being alone?'

I had no idea how to answer that. She baffled me. There was a cold, almost angry look in her eyes, and it scared me. Then she laughed and shook her head.

'Oh, don't pay any attention to me. I'm just babbling.'

When the game was over Ethan and Kenny came right over to us. Ethan looked real cute in his uniform, all dirty with mud and grass stain, and his hat turned around backwards on his head. It was all I could do to keep my eyes off him, but I took Norma's advice and looked at Kenny instead.

Norma smiled at them and said, 'Y'all played a very good game.'

Kenny frowned and shook his head. 'We weren't hitting for nothing. Wish you could have seen us on a better day.'

'Well,' she said, 'I think we got the idea.'

Ethan looked at me and said, 'What did you do to yourself?'

My muscles went rigid. I had almost forgotten about my makeup, and now I didn't have any idea how to explain it.

Norma said, 'It's a good look for her. It brings out her features.'

Ethan squinted, as if trying to locate my features. I looked away.

'Anybody feel like ice cream?' I asked.

'Sounds good. Let's go to Bubba's,' Kenny answered.

Bubba's is this ice cream place right near the church, and it's a big hangout in the summertime. As we started walking, we seemed to fall naturally into twos – Norma and Kenny in front, me and Ethan behind. I wasn't too sure how to go about ignoring Ethan if I was walking right beside him. But after a second I saw I didn't have to worry about that. He didn't have anything to say to me. He just stared at his cleats as they crunched across the gravel.

Bubba's wasn't very crowded, it being a weekday. I could have sworn the lady behind the counter was giving me a strange look, wondering about my makeup. It made me lose my appetite, so I just ordered a Coke.

We sat in a booth, and I just watched them eat their ice cream, wishing I could disappear.

'So what's it like in Richmond?' Kenny asked Norma.

'Oh, it's all right, as cities go.'

'Lots to do, I bet.'

'Enough. Swimming pools and skating rinks and bowling and movies . . . if you like that kind of thing.'

Who wouldn't like that kind of thing, I wondered, but the way she said it made you feel stupid for thinking it was a big deal.

'We used to have a drive-in here,' Ethan said. 'It got blown down in a storm, and they never put it back up.'

'That must have been some storm,' she said.

'Oh, we get some blisters around here in the summer. Real good Dixie storms,' Kenny said proudly.

'What are they?' she asked.

'You know,' he said but then seemed at a loss as to how to explain it. 'Well, like, the kind of thunder that rattles the

whole house. And these long streaks of lightning shoot
across the sky. And trees fall in the road, and people's barns
burn up.'

'Sounds awful,' she said.

'No, it's exciting,' Kenny said. 'Long as it's not your barn
that's burning up.'

'Maybe I'll see a Dixie storm before I leave,' she said,
smiling at Kenny.

'Not likely,' Ethan said. 'We're having a first-class drought.'

'Really?' Norma said, as if a drought was something she'd
always wanted to see.

Ethan nodded. 'Everybody's crops are drying up. My
daddy says his tobacco crop ain't even worth pulling this
year.'

I looked at Ethan. Our eyes met for a second. I wanted
to put my hand on his and say, 'Don't worry, our farm's in
trouble, too. We're in it together.' But I knew I couldn't,
so I looked away.

'Well,' Norma said, 'I don't think it's a good idea to
grow tobacco, anyway. I mean, smoking is so bad for
you. Why do you want to grow something that causes
cancer?'

We all looked at her blankly. Everybody grew tobacco; it
was what we did. It was just a living.

Ethan said, 'What does your daddy do?'

'He works in a bank,' Norma said confidently.

Ethan huffed. 'They're the ones who give us money to
grow tobacco.'

Norma stared at him for a long moment, and for the first time I saw a glimmer of something in her eyes that I never knew was there. She was stumped; she didn't have an answer. It was like seeing the tiniest crack in a wall you thought was solid.

'How did we get on this subject, anyway?' she said. 'What were we talking about before?'

'Storms,' Kenny said.

'That's right. Storms.'

But that was the last anybody said on the subject.

They finished their ice cream, and as we got up to leave I noticed that Kenny and Norma were holding hands. It had happened so suddenly and quietly, like a thing that took no planning at all. What did that mean? Where did that leave Marshall? I thought of Norma's attitude about love and marriage. If those things meant nothing to you, then there probably was no reason not to hold hands with a stranger.

We started up the road, and I was so caught up in my thoughts that I accidentally looked at Ethan when he asked me a question.

'What's wrong with you?'

My mouth dropped open a little. It was too late to pretend I hadn't heard him.

'Nothing's wrong.'

'You're acting kinda weird.'

'I don't think I am.'

I looked up at the trees, concentrating on the big green

leaves that danced overhead, hoping that he might not leave it at that.

But he didn't say another word to me.

Eleven

Norma never told me what was going on between her and Kenny and I never asked. I didn't want to discuss love with her anymore. She seemed to know a lot about it, but the things she knew weren't really the things I wanted to learn.

We got along well for the rest of the week, riding bikes, taking walks, playing card games. Sometimes we included Bodean in our plans, and sometimes we ran off to places where he couldn't find us. I felt a little guilty about that, but there were times when you just didn't want a nine-year-old around.

On Sunday morning I woke up feeling happy and excited. I liked going to church anyway, and I especially liked it when I thought Kenny and Ethan would be there. As I said, they usually didn't come except on Easter and Christmas, but that day I had a feeling they would show up.

I jumped out of bed and nudged Norma. She groaned a little, and her eyes fluttered open.

'What is it?' she said, throwing her arm over her face.

'It's Sunday. You better get up. We're gonna be late for church.'

She took her arm away and looked up at me. 'Church?'

'Yeah. Don't you go to church?'

She shook her head. 'Not in a long time.'

'Why not?'

'I'm an agnostic.'

'Oh. Is that like an atheist?' I'd heard a lot about those, but I'd never really met one.

'No. It's just someone who doubts the existence of God.'

I didn't know what to say to that. It seemed to me everybody doubted the existence of God from time to time. It didn't seem worth giving yourself a title about. I was starting to wonder if there was anything in the world that Norma did believe in.

'Well, we go to church every Sunday. Everybody goes, even Flood.'

She sat up, rubbing her eyes. 'Well, I guess I better go along with the crowd. When in Rome, as they say.'

'Don't your parents go to church?' I asked. This subject had me fascinated.

'My mother does.'

'Not your father?'

'He used to. We all used to. Then when we got home there'd always be a big fight about it. Daddy'd say that the only reason half the people went was to show off their new clothes. Mama said that was better than not going at all. Next thing you knew they'd be yelling about every little thing that ever bugged them . . .'

She laughed after she said this, though I couldn't understand why. 'Then Daddy just stopped going, and Mama went alone.'

'And she doesn't make you go with her?'

'Why would she? I'm old enough to make my own decisions.'

'Yeah, but . . .' I wasn't sure what I was trying to say. The whole thing seemed weird to me.

'Not everybody's family is like yours,' she said out of nowhere.

I didn't know what else to say, and she didn't seem eager to talk anymore, so I started getting dressed. I put on my favorite yellow sundress that tied on the shoulders. It looked good on me, I thought, and I felt pretty secure until Norma came out of the bathroom wearing a black dress that hit her just above the knee and showed off her legs. It was a wrinkled kind of cotton and had an Oriental design around the neck.

'I'm ready as I'll ever be,' she said. Her hair hung loose around her face, dipping over one eye. Her lips were a soft shade of pink. Her triangle earrings were swaying and glimmering in the light.

'Where'd you get that dress?' I asked, almost without knowing it.

'Mama brought it to me from Hong Kong. Daddy went there once on a business trip and took her with him. They used to travel a lot.' She tucked the stray piece of hair behind her ear and said, 'Isn't it appropriate?'

'Sure. It's beautiful,' I said, but in my mind I was

imagining the reactions of the old ladies at church. They still couldn't get used to the fact that women no longer wore hats.

It was too hot to walk to church in our good clothes. We couldn't all fit in Papa's car, so Flood took the truck and let Bodean ride in the back of it. The rest of us piled into the Chevrolet. During the ride Papa and Aunt Macy stared out at the tobacco fields along the way and clucked their tongues sympathetically. Nobody's crop looked any better than ours.

Sure enough, Kenny and Ethan were both at church. Kenny couldn't take his eyes off Norma. As we walked down the aisle to our pew, you could almost hear the heads turning toward us.

Kenny and Ethan sat in the back row with the other kids. Norma and I sat with the family since that was one thing Papa insisted on. He thought the whole point of going to church was for families to worship together. Norma sat between me and Flood. Bodean sat on the other side of me and kept leaning over to whisper things to Norma.

'See that old lady up there with the blue hair? She's got about a million cats. That boy in the front row's retarded. Wait till you see the preacher. He's fat!' Finally Papa told him to be quiet, and he slumped against my arm and pouted.

From where I was sitting I could smell Flood's after-shave, and I noticed he was wearing his best white shirt and a new salmon-colored tie. Norma sat with her hands folded in her lap, occasionally pulling her skirt back down around her knees when it crept up.

The preacher's sermon was about faith, and it had to do mostly with rain. That was all he had preached about, in one form or another, for the past month. The first part was all about how terrible things were, how hard it was to have faith during a drought, and the second part was how we should have faith anyway. Noah didn't lose faith, Job didn't, and Moses didn't. I was a little tired of hearing about those guys. And how did he know they didn't lose faith? They probably lay awake tossing and turning just like everybody else.

When we all bowed our heads, I prayed for rain and for Ethan . . . I wasn't sure what I wanted from Ethan, but I figured maybe God would know.

When service was over, we stood on the lawn for a while, socializing. Papa introduced Norma around, and I noticed people looking at her dress as if it worried them a little. Bodean was rolling around in the grass with some boys his age, and Flood stood off to the side, smoking a cigarette.

I noticed a bunch of older girls standing near him, looking in his direction and whispering. Finally one of them made her way over to Flood. It was Lucy Cabbot, the one Aunt Macy said had called him a while ago. They exchanged a few words. She rocked on her feet as she talked, tucking the same dark strand of hair behind her ear over and over again. Flood smoked his cigarette and nodded occasionally. I was dying to know what they were saying, but before I could listen, I heard a voice close behind me.

'I reckon you're still not talking to me,' it said. I turned and saw Ethan standing there in a dark blue suit with a red tie. The tie and the sun together made his hair look even redder. His eyes were a crisp blue. He looked so cute that it caught me off guard, and I smiled at him.

'Hi,' I said.

'Can I talk to you?'

'I don't see why not.'

He took my arm and led me away from everybody. It felt strange to have his hand around my elbow, guiding me the way I'd seen men guide their wives out of a room.

When we were under the shade of a magnolia tree he said, 'I just want to know what I did.'

'What do you mean?'

'You act like I've got something contagious.'

'I do not.'

'Well, something's wrong because you're sure not acting like yourself.'

'It's probably just your imagination.' I paused and tried to think what Norma would say under these circumstances. 'And besides, you don't really know me all that well.'

He wrinkled his forehead.

'I've known you all my life.'

I didn't answer that so he said, 'Didn't we used to be friends? I mean, at school . . . didn't we used to talk to each other? We had the same lunch period last year. We had Spanish class together.'

'Until you dropped out,' I accused him. He was the

whole reason I took the class, and when he dropped out I took it personally.

'Well, it was confusing. I couldn't understand it.'

'You're not supposed to understand a foreign language. That's the whole point. If you'd stayed in, you'd understand it now. I can say whole sentences in Spanish.'

'Like what?'

'Like . . . "*Hola, Miguel. ¿Donde está mi hermano?*" '

'What does that mean?'

'If you want to know so bad you should take Spanish.'

He smiled. 'That's more like it.'

'More like what?'

'You. Now you're acting like yourself.'

That startled me. I hadn't meant to act like myself. It just happened. I was trying to think of a way to recover when I heard Flood calling across the lawn, telling Papa he was going to head on home. Papa nodded and went on talking.

'So,' Ethan continued. 'You coming to Blue Hole today?'

'I don't know.'

'Jimmy Grogan's bringing a kayak up there. Know what that is?'

'No, I don't and I don't care.' The mere mention of a Grogan made me mad.

I watched Flood as he walked toward his truck. Then I saw that he wasn't alone. At first I was afraid it was Lucy, but when I looked again I saw that Norma was following behind him. He opened the door for her and helped her into the passenger seat. Then he got in the other side, started the truck, and eased out into the road.

I stood there looking at it as it drove away. From behind, the sight was very familiar. It looked the way Flood and Becky used to look riding in the truck together. Him at the wheel and her sitting close beside him.

'. . . I used to think you were okay,' Ethan was saying.

I looked at him. 'What?'

He frowned. 'Aren't you listening to me?'

'I'm sorry. Say it again.'

'Aw, never mind.'

He turned and walked away.

Twelve

That night as we got ready for bed, I asked Norma where she and Flood went after church.

'Oh, nowhere. He just took me riding around. Marston's bigger than I thought it was. There's so much open space.'

'Papa would have taken us riding around.'

She looked up from painting her toenails.

'Is something wrong?'

'No. It's just . . . I guess I thought I'd be the one to show you around Marston.'

'Well, you showed me Blue Hole and softball. Flood figured since he had the truck, he'd just take me . . .' She stopped halfway through and gave me a curious look. 'Are you jealous?'

'What?' I asked, my voice shaking a little.

'I mean about me spending time with somebody besides you.'

'No. Of course not.'

'It doesn't mean I like you less. You've got a way of being possessive with people.'

'I do not.'

'Sure you do. The way you're saving up Flood for his ex-wife.'

'I am not.'

'And the way you're so protective of Bodean. I see how uptight you get when anybody teases him.'

'I have to look after him,' I said, feeling flustered.

She shrugged and said, 'You can't own people, you know.'

'I never thought I could.'

The next day I woke up with a feeling that I wanted to be alone. I almost never felt like that, and I didn't know what to make of it. But as I lay in bed, staring at my same old walls and furniture, I suddenly found myself wishing for another life.

I saw the sunlight streaming in, hot and heavy already, and I knew the crops were still drying up and Papa was still worried. I knew I'd do my chores and the house would be stifling and close, and Aunt Macy would probably have a lie-down headache. Bodean would be obnoxious, Flood would be grumpy, and Norma would just be Norma. I hadn't felt the same about her since she got in the truck with Flood.

It wasn't really what she said, that I was jealous. It was just that image of Flood sitting close to a girl who wasn't Becky. It made me remember the days when she was still here and life was a little bit more normal. Days when she and Flood used to sit together on the porch, laughing as they watched Bodean chase a ball across the yard. She always

94

put her hand on his knee. Sometimes he'd put his arm around her. The farm was thriving in those days, too. Papa always came in from the fields whistling. Aunt Macy cooked a lot in those days and didn't fiddle with her hair so much. It made me remember all those things and how fast we were moving away from them.

As I dragged myself out of bed I started to wonder . . . how do things start to go bad? Is there a certain moment when it all starts? Is there a sign you can recognize as the beginning of the bad days? And once things get bad, do they ever get good again?

Norma slept late while I did the kitchen chores, and when she got up she went right in the living room and started watching talk shows. She had a real passion for talk shows. She talked back to the screen, as if the people could hear her, and she seemed to be an expert on every subject . . . from abortion and low-income housing to breast implants and women who marry prisoners. Bodean sat near her and listened to her every word.

'I can't believe how stupid people can be sometimes,' she said as I dusted the furniture. 'I wish I could have my own talk show. I'd say, "Well, if you're dumb enough to marry a prisoner, you get what you're asking for."'

'Are you gonna be a talk show lady?' Bodean asked. He thought every word from her mouth was gospel.

'Maybe. It's one of my fantasies.'

'What are your other ones?'

'Oh, I don't know. To be an Olympic gymnast. Though

I think maybe my ship has sailed on that one. Sometimes I think I'd like to be a politician. Or a journalist. Something important.'

'I think you ought to be an actress,' Bodean suggested.

'Well, there's always *that*,' she said, as if it were some kind of last resort.

'Move your feet,' I said to him. He had them planted on the coffee table and was leaving all manner of smudge marks.

'Why don't you make me,' he snarled.

'You work too hard, Dutch,' Norma said. 'Why don't you just sit back and enjoy yourself for a few minutes?'

'Somebody's got to do the work.'

Her face fell a little. 'I offered to help.'

I just shrugged. I hadn't remembered her offering to help. She was always taking credit for things she hadn't really done or said.

'Don't pay no attention to her,' said Bodean. 'She's an old grumpy pants.'

'Bodean!' Aunt Macy yelled from the kitchen. 'Come in here and let me cut your hair!'

'Aw, hell. I don't want no haircut,' Bodean grumbled as he walked out.

'Is something wrong, Dutch?' Norma asked when he had gone. 'You seem like you're mad at me.'

'I'm not.'

'Can we go to Blue Hole later? I told Kenny we might be there today.'

'I don't know. I've got a lot of work.'

'Oh, well,' she said, standing and stretching her arms over her head. 'Then I guess I'll just go out for a walk.'

She moved toward the TV set where a bunch of blank-faced women were listening to someone talk about birth control. She turned it off, and their faces flickered, then faded out.

I went upstairs to do my cleaning and decided to start with Flood's room. That was always the worst, and I thought I should go ahead and get it over with. His bedroom used to belong to Mama and Papa, but Flood and Becky took it after they got married. Now that Becky was gone it didn't seem like Flood needed all that space, but he stayed there anyway.

Flood was the real messy type, and I had to pick up all his clothes off the floor and put them away. He dropped them there whether they were clean or not, and I had to smell them to see if they needed to go in the hamper, which wasn't a very enjoyable task. It was a little less terrible because I was related to him, but it made me wonder what cleaning up would be like when I was married. Would I ever get used to handling some strange man's underwear and socks?

I stripped Flood's sheets off and started putting on new ones. He was very fussy about his sheets and didn't like the ones with flowers and frills. He only wanted white or blue. He claimed the other kind gave him nightmares. As I was tucking the fitted sheet under the mattress, my hand hit something sharp, and I drew back with a little gasp. I imagined it was a knife, but on second look I saw it was just a piece of paper. And on the third look I saw it was an envelope.

I stood looking at it, a corner sticking out like the head of an arrow, and I couldn't help wondering . . . what's an envelope doing there? Could it have gotten there by mistake? I stood there for what seemed like a long time, looking at that little piece of pink, wondering what to do about it. I could tuck it back under along with the sheet and forget about it. But that just wasn't in my nature.

What worried me was that it might be a love letter from one of the girls at church, like Lucy. I had to know; it was as simple as that, and I don't pretend to have a better reason for reading his personal mail. I opened the envelope and pulled out a card that smelled faintly of perfume.

It had a picture of a road and some trees, and it said, 'Coming to you from miles away . . .' I cautiously opened it and read on. 'To wish you joy on your special day. Happy birthday with love.' And it was signed, 'Mama.'

For a strange second I thought Mama was sending Flood birthday cards from beyond the grave, or maybe it was an old one from long ago, even though the paper looked brand new. I looked back at the envelope and read the return address: 1919 Alabaster Road, Norfolk, Virginia. Who in the world did we know from Norfolk? Then I read the address, and what I saw nearly stopped my lungs from expanding. It wasn't addressed to Flood at all. It said, clear as day, Bobby Dean Peyton, Rt. 3, Box 89, Marston, Virginia.

That was when my hand started to tremble. It all made sense now. This wasn't Flood's mail, and it wasn't Flood's mama. It was Bodean's. And if there was one letter, there had to be more.

I lifted up a corner of the mattress, but it was heavy, and I couldn't see anything except the box springs underneath. I got down on my knees and shoved my arm way up under the mattress, feeling across the bare fabric until my fingers touched something sharp. I grabbed a fistful of letters and pulled them out.

They were all shapes and sizes and colors. All of them were addressed to Bobby Dean. Some of them looked old and faded, others looked brand new. They all smelled like perfume, the way I remembered Becky smelling.

I had to sit down on the bed and catch my breath. I wasn't sure how to feel. So many things were rushing at me I didn't know which one to think about first. But suddenly I remembered an incident that had happened last summer. One morning while Flood was in the field, Bodean and I walked up to get the mail, even though that was usually Flood's job. We had ordered a pup tent through a catalogue and were eager to get it. It had arrived that day, and Bodean and I went running excitedly across the field to show everybody what we got. Only when we caught up to Flood, he wasn't very excited.

'Where'd that come from?' he snapped.

'We got it in the mail. Look, Dad, it's got poles and everything, and it ties at the bottom in case it rains.'

Flood glared at him and said, 'I don't want you messing around with the mail. You leave that to me. The mail's too important for you to go messing with it.'

'But Dad . . .'

'Bills and things like that . . . if they got lost, we'd be in big trouble. I don't want you ever touching that mail again.'

Bodean and I walked back from the field feeling confused and a little hurt. I couldn't see why we didn't have a right to get the mail. But Flood was a hard person to argue with.

It all came together in a scary, horrible way. And this person I called my brother was someone I felt I didn't even know . . . as if he'd been leading a whole different life apart from us.

With shaky fingers I opened one of the letters and started to read it. I didn't care about betraying Flood anymore; I felt like we were the ones who had been betrayed.

'Dear Bobby Dean,

I'm thinking of you today because it's Easter and I remember the way I used to hide Easter eggs for you on Sunday morning before we went to church. I can recall how your face would light up every time you saw one and you'd come running to me with big eyes and sticky fingers. Halfway through church your stomach would start to hurt from eating all those eggs! I reckon I used to spoil you a little, but I just wanted you to have everything.

It makes me sad that you don't ever write to me. I

know you're old enough to write. Almost nine! You're such a big boy, I probably wouldn't even recognize you! Would you send me a picture? I know you probably don't write because your Daddy doesn't want you to. I don't want you to disobey him but, Bobby Dean, there are some decisions in this world you have to make for yourself. I hope you will think about this and decide what is right in your heart.

I send all my love to you and Papa Earl and Aunt Macy and Dutch. And even to your Daddy, though I expect he doesn't want to hear my name.

Love,
Mama

I was sniffling by the time I put that letter away. I could hear Becky's voice just as plain as day. I could almost hear her humming. I missed her so much my stomach ached.

I hated Flood. I hated him so hard it scared me. It was the first time in my life I really knew what that word meant. It was a cold feeling, and it settled in your bones so deep you thought it might never go away. But the worst part was I couldn't even tell Flood what I knew. After all, I'd been prying around in his business. And that was wrong, no matter how you looked at it.

I wanted to read more, but there were so many letters it would take me a week to get through them all. I knew if I started I'd never stop, so I put the cards and letters back under the mattress and finished making up the bed. Then I sat down to think.

It was a horrible thing to know. I didn't want to own it. But there was no going back, and now I'd have to live forever with this secret. While I sat there trying not to cry I heard footsteps, and my heart froze. I jumped up and looked at the doorway. It was Bodean, with his new haircut.

'What are you doing in my daddy's room?' he demanded.

'Just cleaning.'

'No, you wasn't. You was sitting on his bed.'

'I was taking a rest.'

He thought about this for a second, then said, 'Can't we go to Blue Hole? Norma wants to.'

'Well, why don't you and Norma go? What do you need me for?'

Before he could answer I started smiling. Bodean's head looked all chopped up, and there were cowlicks going in all directions. His freckles showed up bigger, and he looked all bony and frail. He looked like something that hadn't been put together right.

'What's so funny?' he asked, turning red.

'You're a skinhead, that's what.'

He came at me in a hurry, his fists already flying, but I grabbed his arms and looked down at him. He blinked at me curiously, and without thinking I gave him a big hug and kissed the top of his head. He wriggled away, wiping the kiss out of his hair.

'What'd you do that for?' he whined, as if I had spit on him.

'Go on now, so I can finish my work.'

He puffed his cheeks up and walked out, shaking his head.

'Girls,' he said.

Thirteen

After supper we played croquet in the backyard. Bodean was being impossible, trying to show off for Norma. The more he tried to play like a pro, the more he messed up. He pouted and whined and kept asking if he could take his shots over.

'That wouldn't be fair,' Papa said gently but firmly.

Bodean pouted. 'Aw, that won't my real shot. That was just practice. Let me hit again.'

Flood said, 'Bodean, you can't be a baby all your life. If you're gonna play with grownups, you have to act like one.'

'I ain't a baby,' Bodean whined.

'Then shut your yap and let us play.'

Bodean threw down his mallet and stormed to the house. Flood called him a quitter, but Bodean just yelled over his shoulder, 'Make me an offer!'

Papa quit shortly after that, saying his back was giving him trouble. We tried to talk Aunt Macy into taking his place, but she refused. She sat in a lawn chair, fanning herself with a magazine, nursing her heat headache.

I wasn't feeling too jolly myself. I was still upset about those letters, and every time I looked at Flood I felt an attack of anger that settled in my knees and made them quiver. I had also been thinking about Becky and was starting to get annoyed with her. She was the one who left Bodean in the first place, and now she thought a bunch of letters was going to solve everything. The whole situation was one big mess, and it turned me into a grump. It seemed like everybody and everything in the entire world was getting on my nerves.

Norma was top on the list of aggravations. I couldn't stand how happy and giggly she was, flirting shamelessly with Flood. She pretended not to know how to swing the croquet mallet and kept asking him to show her the right way. He was quick to oblige, standing behind her and putting his arms around her in order to demonstrate. She was the world's slowest learner, and he was the world's most patient teacher. They didn't even notice when I walked away.

When I came into the kitchen Papa was standing at the window, watching the sky. I stood beside him and did the same. Without saying anything he put his arm around my shoulders, and we stood together, silently staring at the sun as it made its lazy descent behind the trees. After a second there was a bright flash of light across the horizon. I sucked in a quick breath.

Papa patted my shoulder. 'Just heat lightning. It won't amount to much.'

'Maybe it'll rain.'

'Not for a while, I'm afraid.' He was quiet for a long moment, then said, 'We sure could use one of those Dixie storms, Dutch.'

I nodded, remembering what those storms were like. Even though I knew we needed one, I still dreaded it a little. They always scared the tar out of me. Becky used to let me sit on her lap during those storms. She said if we sang a song, we wouldn't be so afraid. She had a voice like warm butter, and pretty soon I would just fall asleep. The next time I opened my eyes it would be morning, and I would be in my bed, and the storm would be long gone. In those days I believed she had some power to make bad things go away.

After Becky left my fear of storms got worse. I felt like the universe was out of control. Papa tried to explain that they were just God's way of clearing the air. He would take me to the window and make me look at the lightning. He said once you learned to look at it, nothing was as scary. I finally learned how to hide my fear, but the fear itself never really left.

I went to the refrigerator and poured myself a glass of iced tea. Papa stayed by the window, and I sat at the kitchen table, looking at him. After a second I said, 'Papa, can I ask you a question?'

'Of course you can.'

I stared at the ice floating around in my glass and tried to get my words together.

'If you know something . . . a secret . . . and you know somebody has done something wrong . . .' I hesitated, looking up at him. He was listening, undisturbed. 'Well, you know you should tell, but the way you found out wasn't exactly fair. In fact, it was kind of sneaky.' I paused again to

107

swallow. 'What should you do? Should you tell it or keep it to yourself?'

Papa thought about this. He looked at the floor, then back at me. 'I suppose that depends. Would this secret hurt somebody?'

'Well, it would hurt one person and make another person happy.'

Again he thought, then walked over and sat down beside me. I could tell he wanted some details, but the good thing about Papa was that he'd never make me tell more than I wanted to.

'Maybe the best thing to do is just listen to your own conscience.'

I tried to locate my conscience, but it was just as mixed up as the rest of me.

'I snooped,' I told him suddenly. 'I stuck my nose where it didn't belong.'

Papa nodded. 'Well, then, maybe you'd just better keep it to yourself. There are certain things in this world that people weren't meant to know.'

That was just what I thought he'd say. But that meant I had to carry this secret around in my heart, and it was starting to get a little heavy.

Papa looked down and studied his hands for a moment. I looked at them, too. They were big and strong, a little worn from working. They were tanned and freckled and stained with tobacco gum. But they were the nicest hands I had ever seen.

Papa sighed and said, 'Now that you've told me about your secret, I have to tell you one.'

'What?' I asked, my heart fluttering.

'We have to take special care of our girl, Norma.' He hesitated, then said, 'She's going to be having a hard time soon. She's about to face something very difficult . . .'

He raised his eyes to me. 'Her mama and daddy are getting a divorce.'

I felt my mouth dropping open a little. All kinds of things started rushing at me, like when you open a closet that's too full and the contents tumble down on your head. I was sorry I had gotten so annoyed with her. I was sorry I hadn't been a little more understanding.

'She doesn't know yet?' I asked.

He shook his head. 'I just found out today.'

I looked at the sky through the window, just as another flash of heat lightning lit up the world. Outside I could hear Norma and Flood laughing.

'What's she gonna do?'

'She and her mama are going to move to North Carolina. That's where Fran's from, somewhere near Charlotte.' He paused, then added, 'I never even met Fran. She seems nice on the phone.'

I thought carefully before asking my next question.

'What's Uncle Eugene gonna do?'

Papa shook his head. 'I don't know.'

Aunt Macy came in from the yard, rubbing her forehead.

'You'd think it would cool off once the sun went down, but it don't.'

She stopped and looked at us. Her face turned serious and worried.

'You told her?' she asked, and Papa nodded. Aunt Macy sat down and patted my hand.

All of a sudden I started to cry. I didn't mean to, but it just happened. Aunt Macy kept on patting my hand.

'Why do people have to get divorced?' I asked, sucking in a sob.

'Lord only knows,' said Aunt Macy.

I wasn't thinking of Norma so much anymore. I was thinking of Flood and Becky, and all those letters hiding under the mattress. I was thinking of Bodean, whose mother was just like a ghost to him, or a legend, some mysterious figure that other people claimed had once existed, even though they couldn't give him any proof.

It didn't make any sense to me that families could just let themselves be shattered like that. That they could slide in and out of each other's lives as easily as strangers. I looked at Papa, and he seemed to be thinking the same thing.

He said, 'Sometimes folks have problems they just can't work out, Dutch. They can't live together for one reason or another.'

I had stopped crying now. My tears evaporated quickly and left my face feeling raw.

'And I reckon sometimes folks just get tired and give up,' he said.

Aunt Macy smoothed the hair out of my face and gave me a kiss on the ear. That was unusual for her. Like Flood, she wasn't big on hugging and kissing.

'Life's a tricky business sometimes, isn't it, Dutch?' she said.

I nodded. Then the three of us sat there in silence, staring at the table, as Norma and Flood's laughter echoed through the still, hot night.

Fourteen

The idea came to me out of nowhere. It just appeared in my brain, and once it was there I couldn't get it to go away.

I took some of Norma's stationery that she used to write to Marshall. She had piles and piles of it, and I didn't think she'd miss one little sheet. I would have used my own, but I had run out sometime around Christmas. I never bought any more because I didn't have many people to write to.

I sat down at the kitchen table while everyone was out. Aunt Macy had taken Bodean into town for new shoes and underwear. The men were in the fields, and Norma had gone out for one of her long walks. The house seemed very still and spooky. The air was as sticky and hot as ever, and the fan in the kitchen just stirred it around a little.

I began to write.

Dear Becky,
How are you? I am fine. I know it's a surprise to be hearing from me after all this time.
Let me tell you a little about myself. I'm fourteen now and probably look pretty much the way you remember, only taller. I'm getting ready to start the ninth

grade. I don't have a boyfriend at the moment, but I'm working on it.

Everyone is fine. This summer my cousin Norma is staying with us. She is Uncle Eugene's daughter. She is very sweet and pretty, and everyone likes her.

The reason I am writing is I have something to tell you. I have reason to believe that Bodean has never gotten any of your letters. I know you have probably tried to write once or twice. Maybe the mail got messed up or something. Bodean thinks you have forgotten about him, but I'm sure that's not true.

Please don't tell anyone I have written to you. I would get in big trouble. Don't ask how I found your address. I have my ways. And please don't write to me. Don't ask me why, I can't tell you. It's just safer this way.

Maybe you could call us up. It's best to call during the day, especially in the afternoon.

Well, that's all I have to say. Please keep this a secret between us. I know I can trust you.

Love,

Margaret Peyton

(Dutch)

My hands were trembling as I folded the letter. I knew I was taking a gigantic risk, and I wasn't sure what for. I just thought Becky ought to know what was going on.

I took a stamp out of Papa's sock drawer and headed for

the mailbox so I could wait for the mailman to come. I wanted to be sure I could put it right in his hands. The mailbox was at the end of our road, and I was hot and sweaty by the time I got there. It was nearly eleven o'clock and that was when he came.

I sat at the edge of the road and watched for his truck. The Grogan boys passed a couple of times and hollered out the window at me. It seemed like they had nothing better to do with their time than waste it. Sometimes I wondered why God bothered to invent people like the Grogans.

Finally the mailman came. He smiled when he saw me.

'You must be expecting something special,' he said. His name was Ernie Grunts. He had a pointed head and crooked teeth. He was almost Papa's age and still lived with his mother.

'Not really,' I said, handing him the letter. 'Just didn't have anything better to do.'

Ernie handed me our mail, which was just some bills and a few catalogues. Aunt Macy was a catalogue nut. She did all her Christmas shopping that way. I glanced at them and put them in our box so Flood wouldn't know I'd been messing with the mail.

When Ernie went on his way I breathed a sigh of relief. I marveled at how my letter could find its way from a guy like Ernie all the way to a woman alone in a city like Norfolk. When I thought about that I had a lot of respect for the postal system.

I walked back feeling happy but a little bit scared, as if I'd set something very big in motion.

A few yards up ahead I saw two people standing next to the cow pasture. They were underneath a shady oak tree, having what looked like a serious discussion. As I got closer I saw that it was Norma and Flood.

My curiosity got the better of me again. I sneaked up near them and stood behind a growth of shrubbery. I could only see them through bare spots in the leaves, but their words came through real clear.

Flood was doing the talking at the moment. He was saying, 'I just think you've got a real active imagination.'

'Why?' asked Norma.

'You're getting carried away.'

'I don't think I'm the only one getting carried away.'

'Norma, come on. You're so young . . .'

'You didn't think I was so young last night.'

'That's just what I mean. Last night was just a little harmless flirting. It didn't mean anything.'

'You kissed me!' she shouted.

'Well, Norma . . . that's nothing.'

'You didn't act like it was nothing.'

'But it is. People like me . . . men my age . . . they don't just go around necking with girls . . .'

'I know what men your age do.'

'For crying out loud, you're young enough to be my daughter!'

'My father is ten years older than my mother.'

'Well, I'm twenty years older than you. You're a kid. You're Dutch's age.'

'Don't compare me to her. We're nothing alike.'

'What have you got against Dutch?'

'Nothing. She's a sweet kid. But that's all she is, a kid. She's not especially mature for her age. She's very limited.'

A sick feeling was growing across my stomach. I should have walked away, but the worse it got, the more I wanted to hear.

Then Flood said, 'Dutch is no fool. She could probably teach you a few things.'

I couldn't believe Flood had defended me. But before I had time to ponder it, Norma started talking again.

'Don't be ridiculous. She doesn't know anything. And when it comes to love, she's hopeless. She thinks it's something out of a fairy tale, the way she sits around pining for that boy, Ethan. She doesn't begin to know how to get what she wants. It's not her fault . . . growing up in a place like this. But I've seen and done things she's only dreamed about. So don't go telling me we're anything alike.'

Flood said, 'That's not the point. We're not talking about Dutch. The fact is, you've got a schoolgirl crush on me. I got carried away and took advantage of it. But I don't intend to take it any farther.'

'I can't believe it. I can't believe last night was a mistake.'

'Well, it was.'

Norma didn't say anything for a long moment. I moved

some branches aside and saw her staring at the ground, shaking her head.

'You're still in love with your wife, aren't you?' she finally asked. 'You're waiting for her to come back.'

'You leave her out of this.'

'Why? It's the truth. You're just waiting for something that's never going to happen. She's not coming back, Flood. You're just living in a dream.'

Then Flood did something that took me by surprise. He grabbed Norma by the shoulders and shook her hard, the way he shook Bodean sometimes for misbehaving.

'Listen, girl. You're getting into dangerous territory. Nobody tells me about my wife. Nobody talks to me like that, you got it? It's not beyond me to slap your face!'

'Do it then!' she shouted. 'I wish you would!'

I wished he would, too. But he just dropped his arms and stared at her. After a moment he looked up at the sky and let out a long, heavy breath.

'I don't know what's happening to me,' he said.

I heard his footsteps going away. After a second Norma let out an exasperated little scream and kicked at the dirt. Finally she started walking back to the house, and I kept still, putting off the moment when I would have to crawl out and try to act normal again.

If I could have stayed behind that bush forever, I would have. But I was learning that one of the hardest things about life is that sooner or later you have to come out from your hiding place.

Fifteen

I took a walk around the farm to let myself cool off. I hurt all over, the way you do when you exercise a bunch of muscles that haven't been used for a long time. It was a real, physical ache, and I wanted to slide into a hot bath and make it go away. I felt old.

I could remember only one time before that I felt this bad. That was the day that Becky left. I wouldn't forget it as long as I lived.

It was a Sunday morning, and when Papa came into my bedroom I thought he was just waking me up for church, even though Aunt Macy was the one who usually did that. He sat down on the edge of my bed, and as I looked up at him, it was the first time I ever noticed those sad lines around his eyes.

He told me, in a soft voice, that Becky had gone away. It didn't make sense to me at first, and I made him repeat it just to be sure I'd heard right. I couldn't believe she would leave so suddenly and quietly. I hadn't even heard them fighting, the way they sometimes did in their room late at night.

I asked when she was coming back, and he said probably not for a long time, if ever.

'Are they getting divorced?' I asked. I had just learned about divorce. Janie Catterwall's parents had just gotten divorced, and it had caused a big stir all over town. Suddenly the teachers were treating Janie a lot nicer, letting her take catnaps during lessons and not minding if she left school early.

'I don't know. Maybe,' he said.

'Did she take Bodean?' The thought of it made me freeze up inside. He was only three then and still cute, all pudgy and dimply in his overalls and little white shoes. He was almost like a toy.

'No,' he said.

I felt relieved, but almost right away I knew there was something wrong with that. How could she do without him? I couldn't imagine life without Bodean, and I wasn't even his mother.

'Why not?' I asked.

'I don't know. I don't know much at all . . . just what Flood told me.'

'Is he upset?'

'Of course he is.'

'Well, why doesn't he go after her?'

He didn't answer that. Instead he stood up and patted my leg through the quilt.

'I know she'll come back,' I told him. 'She has to.'

'We'll see,' he said.

For weeks and even months afterwards, I kept expecting Becky to come back. I'd race home from the bus stop and

120

go running through the house, looking for some sign of her. I'd jump whenever the telephone rang. I'd hurry to the window whenever a car drove down our road. I'd play little games with myself, saying, 'If the sky is cloudy tomorrow, that means Becky is coming back.' This went on for what seemed like a long time. But Becky never came back, and gradually, almost without knowing it, I gave up.

As I walked down the dirt path beside the pasture, I had the same kind of feeling I had during those days. I felt betrayed and abandoned. And what was worse, I felt to blame. If I had been a different person, none of this would have happened.

I walked past the cows, and they just blinked lazily at me. I stuck my tongue out at them, but they went right on blinking. Then I picked up a rock and threw it in their direction. It landed a few feet away with a clunk, but they never moved. It's hard to upset a cow.

I followed the path down to the cornfield where Bodean and I used to play. When I was smaller I could get lost in the corn, so deep that when I looked up I couldn't even see the sky. I couldn't do that anymore. I had gotten bigger, and the corn had gotten smaller.

Norma had said a lot of bad things, but one of the worst was that she told Flood my secret about Ethan. It was the second person she had told. She just tossed it away as if it never even mattered. And I felt like a fool for ever trusting her. She had never meant to be my friend.

Then she said I couldn't know anything because I had

grown up here. Was she right? Was that why I was stupid enough to trust her? Maybe the world was full of people like her, people who didn't believe in anything and who didn't keep their promises.

I wanted to walk off into the cornfield and disappear. In fact, I was contemplating doing just that when I looked up and saw Bodean running toward me, as fast as his skinny little legs would carry him. His face was pinched and worried, his fists clenched tight. He stopped in front of me, panting and patting his chest.

'Something's wrong with Norma,' he blurted out. 'She's crying.'

'Well, big deal. Everybody cries now and then. Especially girls. You ought to know that.'

He shook his head, still catching his breath.

'Her heart is breaking.'

'Is that what she told you?'

He nodded. 'I said, "What's wrong with you?" And she said, "Nothing except my heart is breaking." '

'It's not really breaking, Bodean. That's just a figure of speech.'

'But you should just see her. She's all red in the face. I think we better do something. Maybe we should tell Grandpa.'

'She'll live,' I said bitterly.

'You don't care about her. You don't care about nobody but yourself.'

'That's not true.'

'I hate you!' he screamed.

'Bodean . . .' I said, but he had given up on me. He turned and ran back to the house, just as fast as he had come. I followed him at a slower pace, giving him time to calm down.

When I came into the living room he was absorbed in an afternoon cartoon. I hesitated, thinking he might want to apologize, but he just waved me out of the way and said, 'You make a better door than a window, even if you are a pane.'

I went upstairs to look for Norma. I knew I should have left her alone, but I wasn't that kind of a person. The whole business was nagging at me like a hangnail, and I had to get rid of it, even if it hurt.

When I came into my room, Norma was curled up on her bed, face down, crying into the pillow. She cried quietly, but her whole body shook. I wasn't sure she heard me come in, but after a second she turned over and looked at me. Her face was all puffy, and her eyes were streaked and red. Strands of hair were sticking to her wet cheeks. Suddenly she didn't look special to me. She looked like an ordinary girl.

She said, 'Dutch, if you don't mind, I'd really like to be alone.'

'This is my room,' I snapped.

'Well, yes, if you want to get technical.' Then she turned over and cried some more.

I sat down on my bed and looked at her for a long time before speaking.

'What's wrong?' I finally asked.

She sat up, wiping at her face and trying to smile.

'Just another one of my moods.'

'Is that so?'

She raised her eyebrows. 'Why are you taking that tone?'

'What tone?'

Our eyes locked. I could almost hear her brain working, and I tried to keep my face still. Should I tell her what I knew? Or should I just let her figure it out?

'I guess I miss Marshall . . .' she said slowly. 'Is there anything so unusual about that?'

'You don't miss people, remember?'

She blinked at me curiously. I thought I saw a little bit of fear in her face.

'Are you accusing me of something?'

'A guilty conscience needs no accusing.' That was something Aunt Macy said about once a day.

'And just what am I guilty of?'

'Lying,' I answered. 'You're crying about Flood.'

It came out, just like that. I knew I was in deep now and there was no turning back. Her face went blank, and the tears suddenly stopped.

'What makes you think that?' she asked. I didn't answer; I didn't have to. She could see it in my eyes.

'You little sneak! You were listening to us!'

'You're the sneak, Norma. After you made me think you liked me . . .'

124

'Well, you know what they say. Eavesdroppers never hear good things about themselves. That's what you get for listening to a private conversation.'

'I couldn't help it,' I lied, feeling flustered. 'But what you did was just as bad. Those things I told you about Ethan were private. And you just blurted them out. You didn't even care . . .'

'You and your secrets. Do you really think any of that stuff matters? You think you've got such big problems. You don't even know what problems are.'

She buried her face in her hands again and cried very loud. Her tears didn't move me at all. I felt cold inside.

'You're the one who thinks you're so important,' I said. 'Like nobody in the world matters but you. You think you should have everything you want, don't you?'

She didn't answer. She just went on crying. I couldn't think of anything else to say, so I stood up and went to the door. But just as I got there, her voice stopped me.

'I just want somebody to need me. I don't think that's a lot to ask.'

I turned and looked at her. She was staring away from me, toward the wall, as if speaking to an invisible person.

'I thought you were on a solo mission in life. That's what you said.'

'No. That's what my father said. That's what everybody thinks. Norma's fine, Norma doesn't need anything, Norma's just perfect. What do they know about me? What does anybody know?' She blew out a breath, still looking at the wall. 'I'm just so tired of it all.'

'What?'

She turned her head to me. 'Being perfect.'

I wasn't sure what she meant. And truthfully, I wasn't listening anymore. I was thinking of my own problems.

I said, 'For your information, I needed you. And you let me down.'

'You don't even know me,' was her answer.

'I wish you weren't my cousin,' I said angrily.

'I wish the same thing.'

'Good,' I said.

'Fine,' she said.

She looked away from me, and I opened the door. I didn't have anything left to say, but somehow I felt I wasn't finished. I hadn't gotten the best of her yet.

So I turned to her and said, 'I'm glad your parents are getting a divorce.'

Her body stopped quaking and turned rigid. I held onto the doorknob for support. I suddenly heard the sound of my words, and I knew without a doubt it was the worst thing I had ever said.

'What?' she asked quietly.

'You heard me,' I went on, like my tongue didn't even belong to me. 'Your parents are getting a divorce. And I don't blame them. You're probably the reason.'

When she looked at me, her face was flushed, and there were tears in her eyes – real tears that came from somewhere deep. They spilled over onto her cheeks and slid down around her chin.

I had finally hurt her enough.

Sixteen

No one said anything about Norma's absence at supper. Everyone seemed absorbed in their own worries. Papa had had another visit from the men at the bank, and his face had that dull, distracted expression it always got when something was weighing on him. Flood didn't eat much and just sat there smoking one cigarette after another. Aunt Macy kept waving the smoke away with one hand and twisting her hair with the other. Bodean was still mad at me and wouldn't even pass me the salt. I left the table as soon as I could and decided to worry about the dishes later.

I sat on the front porch, reading a library book until it got too dark to see. Then I just stared out at the lightning bugs, quick yellow dots in the darkness, and the bats swooping in crazy circles around the streetlight before disappearing toward the stars.

Flood came out eventually and stood on the porch, staring out at the yard. He didn't see me at first, and when he did he jumped a little, then laughed quietly.

'You scared me,' he said.

I shrugged and looked down at my book, which was still open in my lap.

'You're gonna ruin your eyes,' he said.

'I'm not really reading.'

'What is that?' he asked, meaning the book.

'*Huckleberry Finn.*'

'Oh, yeah. I remember that,' he said, as if talking about something that happened a long time ago. 'I can't tell you the last time I read a book.'

He walked over to me and stood close by. He smelled like after-shave. When I looked up at him, I saw that he was wearing a crooked smile.

'It's funny, isn't it? The way things change.'

'What kind of things?'

'I was just thinking. When you're young, you think you're going to last forever. You start believing that nothing ever changes. Then one day you look around and see that they've been changing all along and you were just too close to it to notice.'

'Yeah,' I said, though it sounded like something he didn't expect me to understand.

'When you've got kids around, you can't help noticing they're growing up. Bodean's shooting up like a weed and you're nearly as tall as Macy.' He chuckled. 'Suddenly you have to say, "Wait a minute. If they're getting older, then I must be getting older, too." '

It was strange the way he was talking. I'd never heard Flood say things like that.

'Oh, Dutch,' he said, shaking his head and smiling, as if I'd just said something amusing. 'The world just tosses you around, don't it? It just won't let you sit still.'

'Who wants to sit still?' I asked, but he didn't hear me. He didn't even seem to be talking to me. He was talking to the night.

Then he threw his jean jacket over his shoulder and walked off toward his truck. I could hear his boots, crunching on the gravel. I watched as he got into the truck and started it up. The lights popped on, sending two yellow beams across the grass. Then the truck pulled out in a cloud of dust and moved on down the dark road, the taillights staring at me like evil red eyes.

I dozed off in the rocking chair, but it was a shallow sleep, and I was aware of all the night sounds. They moved into my dreams and made me imagine I was lost in the woods, with crickets chirping and frogs belching and dogs howling in the distance. Then the screen door creaked, and I jerked awake, feeling dizzy.

Papa pulled up a chair beside me and smiled. I tried to smile back, but I felt a lump growing in my throat, and I had to pause to swallow it back down. Finally he put his hand on my arm and said, 'Tell me about it, Dutch.'

'Tell you what?'

'I know when something's bothering you.'

'Oh.' I thought about denying it, but I didn't want to. I couldn't keep a secret from him for very long. I tried to pick the right words, but when I opened my mouth they just darted out carelessly, 'Papa, I've done a terrible, horrible thing.'

'Do you want to tell me what?'

'You're going to hate me.'

'Don't talk nonsense, Dutch. Just go on and tell me.'

I swallowed that lump again.

'I told Norma about her parents. About the divorce.'

I looked at him. He didn't seem so much mad as disappointed.

'I asked you to keep that a secret,' he said.

'I'm sorry.'

'Her mama was going to tell her on the phone tomorrow.'

'I don't know what came over me.'

He sighed. 'What's done is done, I reckon.'

'That's not all. I didn't just tell her. I said it in a mean way.'

His forehead wrinkled. I hated that confused look on his face, as if he couldn't imagine why I would do something mean.

'I wanted to hurt her,' I explained.

'Why?'

'Because I heard her saying some bad things about me. It just made me so mad, I lost my head.'

I stopped short of repeating my exact words. I couldn't bring myself to say them again.

'Anyhow, I didn't really mean what I said. At least I don't think I did.'

Papa rubbed his chin. 'Well, you're just going to have to apologize.'

I shook my head. I couldn't even think of facing Norma.

'I reckon I'm just bad,' I said. 'Just like Flood. I've got the devil in me.'

'I guess we all do from time to time. Folks say things in anger . . . it's like a monster that takes over your mouth. It's wrong, but everybody does it.'

'Well, nobody is as mean as I am.'

'Now, Dutch,' Papa said in a scolding voice. 'Everybody's got faults, but it don't do any good to start glorifying them.'

I stared at him. I had no idea I was doing that.

'That's just another form of conceit,' he went on, 'being proud of your failings. It's easy to throw your hands up and say, "Well, I'm just bad." And it's easy to sit back and get lazy, thinking you're as good as they come. The hard part's looking yourself straight in the eye and realizing you're a little bit of both.' He paused and then asked, 'Do you know what I mean?'

I shrugged.

'You've got a conscience. You know when you've done something wrong. What you did to Norma was wrong, plain and simple.'

'I thought she deserved it,' I said. Now that I had gotten it all off my chest I felt a little bit defensive.

'Well, it's not up to you to decide something like that. Vengeance is a terrible thing.'

'It belongs to the Lord,' I said, recalling the scriptures and wondering why God got to have all the satisfaction.

'I don't think the Lord is interested in vengeance, Dutch.

133

He just wants folks to get along, I reckon.'

I thought about that, then said, 'What should I do?'

'Apologize to Norma. That's all you can do.'

I swallowed, and I could still feel the residue of anger somewhere inside me, like the sticky film that orange juice sometimes leaves across your throat.

'Even if I don't entirely mean it?' I asked.

'Even if you don't mean it,' he said, 'because one day soon you will mean it.'

He leaned over and patted my knee. 'Go on, now.'

I stood up. My legs were wobbly. I turned and went into the house, feeling like this was the hardest thing I'd ever have to do.

She was writing in her journal when I came in, just as she was the first night she stayed with us. I closed the door quietly, and she pretended not to notice me. Finally I said, 'Norma.'

'Hmmm?' Eventually she looked up with a faint smile.

'I'm sorry about what I said. It was wrong.' My voice stalled in the middle of the apology. I'd hoped it would be longer and more graceful, but suddenly I wanted to leave it at that.

She shrugged. She had combed her hair and put on makeup. Her face was as still as a painting.

'That's all right,' she said. Then she went back to writing. I stood there watching her, still unsatisfied.

'Aren't you mad at me?'

'Well, Dutch, if you want to know the truth,' she said

slowly, 'I just don't care enough to be mad.'

Of all the things she could have said, that was the worst. I felt as if she'd cut my legs out from under me.

'If there's one thing I've learned in life,' she went on, 'it's that you can't give people the satisfaction of caring about their opinion.'

She paused, writing another sentence in her journal. Then she said, 'And as far as my parents are concerned, you didn't tell me anything I didn't already know. And I don't particularly care about their problems, either. If they want to wreck their lives, it's their business.'

'But they're your parents!' I said stupidly. 'And it's your life, too.'

She laughed. 'Well, it depends on how you look at it.'

I stared at her face, which was so calm and unperturbed. Her 'attitude' had taken over again. But the thing was, I didn't buy the attitude anymore. I had seen her without it.

'I don't believe you're not upset,' I said.

She sighed and threw her pen down. 'Why can't you just leave me alone? Why can't anybody leave me alone?'

I didn't answer. She picked up her pen again and went back to writing. I could see the discussion was over, and I could see that it hadn't accomplished very much. She was still mad at me, and I was still mad at her.

Norma closed her journal at last, and without even asking me she switched off the light. I took off my jeans and got into bed with my T-shirt still on. My whole body felt rigid, like a clenched fist. I tried to remember the feeling I used to have right before I went to sleep at night . . . snug and sure, with the notion that everything was safe. I wondered if I would ever feel that way again.

Not long after I dozed off, I was awakened by a racket on the stairs. I sat straight up in bed, my heart pounding. I looked over at Norma, but she was sound asleep.

I crept out of bed and hurried over to the door. I cracked it just a little. There was a light on the stairs, and I saw two figures coming up, swaying from side to side. It was Aunt Macy and Flood. Flood was doing most of the swaying, and Aunt Macy was just trying to keep him on his feet. He was as drunk as I'd ever seen a person.

'Leave me here,' Flood said in a slur, like his mouth was full of glue. 'I'll just sleep here.'

Aunt Macy whispered, 'Keep quiet, Flood. Stop talking foolishness.'

'I don't give a damn. I don't give a damn.'

'Stop swearing. Isn't it enough you're drunk?'

'I just don't give a damn.'

'If your father saw you like this, he'd turn you out into the street. He doesn't want nothing to do with drunkenness in this house. Stand up straight, Flood! I swear, you're going straight to hell.'

Flood laughed out loud. It made me jump back.

'How will I know when I get there?' he said. 'How will I tell the difference?'

I closed the door quietly. I was sweating all over, but my hands felt as cold as ice.

Seventeen

One evening while we were washing up the supper dishes, Bodean said to me, 'You don't like Norma no more.'

It wasn't a question. It was something he just knew. I supposed he had noticed that we didn't do things together anymore. She usually spent the days watching one talk show after another, then going for long walks or practicing her gymnastic stunts on the lawn. Sometimes Kenny would drop by to see her, and I watched them from the window as they sat under the hickory tree, talking and laughing. I kept on with my chores and sometimes rode my bike. I always thought to ask her if she wanted to go along, but she said no.

'Bicycling is really not my best sport,' she said pleasantly, but we both knew what was underneath. We had broken up, the way sweethearts do. The attraction was gone, and now it was just awkward trying to get along, knowing things weren't the way they used to be.

When Bodean said that, I stared into the soapy water and pretended not to hear him.

'You made her mad,' he went on.

'Oh, really? How did I do that?'

'I don't know. But if she leaves here, it's gonna be your fault.'

'You always knew she had to leave one day.'

'She might stay longer if you didn't act so mean.' He was drying off a coffee cup, wiping hard at it like he was trying to get the paint to come off.

'That's not fair.' I sighed. I was trying to be patient with him.

'Maybe you're the one who ought to leave.'

'Maybe you're right.'

Bodean didn't want to hear that. He wasn't in the mood to be agreed with. All of a sudden he flung that coffee cup up against the wall, and it shattered into little pieces. I just looked slowly over at him. He stared up at me with big, teary eyes.

'Now go on and tell my daddy,' he said and darted out of the room, slamming the back door behind him.

Aunt Macy came in the kitchen while I was sweeping the pieces up.

'What in the world happened?' she asked with a worried expression. She didn't like a mess.

'I guess I got clumsy.'

'I don't know what's happening around here,' she said.

I didn't know either, and I didn't like to think about it much. Norma and I were dodging each other, Bodean was starting to hate me, and Flood seemed to be sliding down, turning into a person none of us even recognized. He went out every night and came in late, usually drunk. One night

I heard him and Papa yelling at each other, but I covered up my ears so I wouldn't have to hear. I was tired of listening to other people's conversations.

The drought was getting worse. Tobacco wasn't all that was suffering. We didn't eat fresh vegetables anymore. Instead we got the frozen ones from last summer, the ones we usually ate only in winter. It was a horrible feeling, the first day I went down to the basement with Aunt Macy to get some corn for supper. We opened the freezer, and a rush of cold smoke hit me in the face. I stared at all those white containers with the dates of last summer written on them, and I felt like crying. I couldn't help thinking, 'What will become of us? What happens to people when their food runs out?' It was a question I'd never asked myself before.

Suddenly I had this vision of my whole family standing in the free cheese line at the courthouse on Tuesdays. Or me and Bodean getting free lunch tokens at school, like those kids we always stared at with curiosity and a little bit of fear. Or, what was worse, I could see Papa loading us and all our belongings into the truck and driving us off to a city full of strangers.

Aunt Macy saw my expression and seemed to read my mind. She said, 'Well, things always turn out somehow. We made it through the Depression, don't forget.'

That cheered me up a little bit because I liked the stories of the Depression – how everybody pitched in together and saved things, and all sat together in front of the fire at night, telling stories and trying to keep warm. But then I realized that the Depression was different. That happened to the whole country. And this just seemed to be happening to a little pocket of people in a forgotten corner of the world.

That night after Bodean broke the coffee cup, some clouds began to gather in the sky. They were big and purple and swollen, and to me they looked beautiful. We all sat on the front porch and watched them lining up like rocks in the sky. But after a while they just broke apart and scattered, until there were only purple splinters left behind.

The next morning at breakfast Papa made an announcement.

He waited till everyone had pushed back their plate, except for Bodean who always had a hard time at breakfast. He didn't like eggs or bacon or oatmeal, and it was a struggle for him to hide the food on his plate.

Papa said, 'Well, I got a couple of pieces of news. Not too good, I'm afraid.'

Flood lit a cigarette and squinted, picking little pieces of tobacco off his tongue. Aunt Macy raised her napkin to her mouth, as if to stifle a sound.

Papa said, 'First of all, I hope y'all haven't got too attached to that old tractor out there 'cause after next week it won't belong to us anymore.'

Bodean looked up from his mangled eggs. 'What are you talking about?'

'They're coming to take it away,' Flood said sternly. His prediction had come true and he seemed slightly proud.

'Who is?' Bodean demanded. 'That's our tractor! We paid

for it! Even if it is an old piece of crap,' he added for his father's benefit. I thought Flood might pop him for swearing, but he just gave Bodean a crooked, appreciative smile.

'Unfortunately we hadn't paid for all of it,' Papa said. 'And the men at the bank want it back.'

'Aw, hell,' Bodean said, feeling brave now. 'How we gonna pull tobacco without a tractor?'

'We'll manage somehow,' Papa said, and his answer seemed to annoy Flood. He smirked and shook his head before taking a sip of coffee.

'I knew this day was coming,' Aunt Macy said, staring at her plate. 'I could feel it.'

'Now, Macy, it ain't the end of the world,' Papa said with a little chuckle. 'I've had equipment repossessed before and always got it back somehow.'

'That was only in the beginning,' Aunt Macy insisted. 'In the early days.'

Bodean threw his fork down and said, 'Dammit all!'

'You better watch that mouth,' Papa said angrily.

Flood just went right on smoking, as though Bodean's mouth wasn't much of his concern. Bodean shot a look at Norma, who had kept herself quiet the whole time, cutting her bacon into tiny pieces before eating it.

Then Papa said, 'And the other sad news is that our girl is gonna be leaving us soon.'

Norma looked up then and gave us all a small smile. Her eyes fell on me for a second, but I couldn't stand it and I looked away.

Bodean's face turned bright red and he said, 'Well, that just does it.'

'We're all sorry to see her go,' Papa agreed.

'How come she has to leave?' Bodean demanded.

'Because her mama wants her back,' said Papa. 'And you can't blame her for that.'

Norma said, 'Everyone has been very nice, and I've enjoyed myself.' It sounded like something she had rehearsed.

Bodean said, 'Why can't we send Dutch away and keep Norma?'

Everybody at the table laughed except me and Bodean. He was dead serious, and I was half afraid someone would take him up on the suggestion.

Flood fixed his eyes on the wall and said, 'When are you going?'

Norma looked at him, staring hard. She was waiting for his eyes to come around to her, but they never did.

'Day after tomorrow.'

Flood just nodded and blew out a stream of smoke,

'We're sure gonna miss you, Norma,' Aunt Macy said. She hesitated, as if she wanted to say something else. Then she just threw her napkin down and left the table. Everyone was quiet for a second. Her absence left us all feeling a little unbalanced.

'I'm gonna miss y'all, too,' Norma said.

That was enough for Bodean. He jumped up from the table and ran out, barely escaping before the tears came. I could hear him howling by the time he reached the back porch.

Papa said, 'Well, you can always come back for a visit. You're family, and family always sticks together, don't they?'

Flood shook his head with a laugh.

'Yeah, that's right. Family is forever, ain't it?' He stubbed his cigarette out in his plate and stood up.

Norma said, 'I feel like I've just disrupted everything.'

Flood said, 'Naw, that's all right. We were already disrupted.'

He walked out then, leaving only the three of us behind. The table looked lopsided. All those empty spaces made me feel gloomy. Papa started at his lap and let out a little sigh. Finally Norma looked at me.

'I don't guess you'll miss me at all, Dutch,' she said.

It caught me by surprise, and my mouth fell open a little.

Papa raised his eyes to me. I could tell he wanted me to say something back to Norma, but I just didn't know what it would be. My head felt like a clogged drain.

'Well . . .' I said, but nothing else came out. The two of them sat watching me, waiting for the rest.

Then I stood up and left, like all the others.

Eighteen

The night before Norma left we went to a potluck supper at the church. Everybody in town came. All you had to do was bring something to eat, and they'd let you join in. Even the Grogan boys came, carrying a box of store bought cookies.

Mrs. Evans, the potluck organizer, didn't favor that too much.

'Now, Daryl, looks like y'all could've done better than a box of old lemon cookies.'

'Well, we meant to get some Oreos, but they was out,' Daryl said humbly.

She sighed. 'I reckon y'all gonna stay and eat, no matter what I say.'

Daryl just smiled, and he and Jimmy went off to join the festivities.

The supper was held on the lawn. Aunt Macy and I helped the women set everything up and serve the food. Norma wasted no time in locating Kenny, and the two of them went off by themselves, holding hands and talking. Kenny had a serious expression, and Norma looked sad, so I figured she was giving him the news.

As usual Bodean took a big helping of all the food and only ate about two bites.

'Now don't you feel bad?' I asked. 'Here we sit in the middle of a drought, and you're throwing all that food away.'

'Don't taste right,' he said, tossing his paper plate into the trash can. 'It's almost as bad as your cooking.'

I didn't point out that the only thing he ate were the deviled eggs I made.

We sat on the lawn for a while, watching all the folks moving around us. I couldn't help noticing that Flood was talking to some of the women from church. Lucy Cabbot was one of them. She was more dressed up than a person ought to be at a potluck, and I noticed her hair was slightly curled at the ends. She was tucking a strand behind her ear, the way she always did. The thing that got me, though, was that Flood kept nodding while she talked and smiled now and again. He even laughed once, out loud, with his head thrown back. It made my stomach knot up, so I looked away.

Papa stood among a cluster of men, and I could tell they were talking about the weather. It was all anybody his age talked about anymore. One of the men was Ethan's father. He had the same red hair and the same squinty grin.

Bodean said, 'Let's play freeze tag.'

I considered it for a second. Usually I'd oblige him, but I looked over and saw Ethan playing horseshoes with some other guys just a few feet away, and I didn't want him to see me prancing around like a child.

'You can't play with two people,' I told him.

'Let's get Norma.'

'She wouldn't be interested.'

'You're just saying that 'cause you hate her.'

'I don't hate anybody.'

'You ain't any fun no more,' he answered, grabbing for his trusty BB rifle, which he took with him everywhere these days. He pointed it at the sky, as if waiting for a duck to fly overhead.

'Put that thing down. You're gonna hurt somebody.'

'Do me a favor,' he said. 'You ain't my mama.'

Those words made me think about Becky, and I wondered why she hadn't called. Maybe my letter made her mad somehow. Or maybe Ernie Grunts lost it along the way. I couldn't think of a reason she wouldn't at least try to respond . . . unless what Flood said was true, and she just didn't care.

When I looked back at Bodean, he was pointing his gun in Flood's direction.

Bodean squinted his eye down the barrel and said, 'Think I can hit one of those girls on the butt?'

He was aiming at Lucy.

'Stop that, now. I mean it. A gun's not a plaything.'

'It's just dumb old BB's.'

'I don't care. It's dangerous.'

I grabbed the barrel of the gun and lowered it. Bodean pouted.

'When I grow up I'm gonna be a criminal,' he said.

'You're gonna do no such thing.'

'I'm gonna rob banks.'

'What for?' I was getting worried about his tone of voice.

' 'Cause then you don't have to worry about whether it rains. And nobody'll come and take your tractor away.'

'They'll put you in jail.'

'That suits me. There ain't no girls in jail.'

He raised his rifle to his shoulder again and pointed in the direction of Kenny and Norma. At that exact moment Kenny put his arm around Norma, and Bodean turned so red I could have sworn he was going to shoot. I grabbed his gun and pointed it back at the ground.

'I'm gonna wear you out!' I shouted, a little too loud.

'You just try it.'

'Boy,' I said, 'you're gonna bust hell wide open.'

'I don't care if I go to hell,' he proclaimed. 'I'll know a lot of folks down there.'

'Like who?'

'Like you. And my mama.' With that he tucked his rifle under his arm and ran away.

I just let him go. I was getting tired of running after Bodean and trying to steer him on the right course. I was too young to be a mother.

I got up and wandered in the direction of the horseshoe game. I thought I might try to get Ethan to talk to me. I felt bad about taking Norma's advice and ignoring him. Now I had probably made Ethan mad at me for life, and I had no one to blame but myself.

Ethan was pitching as I walked up. His horseshoe sailed through the air and landed a few inches from the stake with a thud. A puff of red dirt rose up and made me cough.

'Pretty good, Ethan,' one of the boys said.

He shook his head. 'I can do better than that.'

His eyes lifted up and landed on me. He stared at me for a second, then looked away. Jimmy Grogan, who was standing nearby, said, 'You wanna have a go, Dutch?'

'Nah, I'm just watching.'

'Girls can't play horseshoes,' Ethan objected.

'This one can,' Jimmy said. 'She doesn't even know she's a girl.'

'She sure does pack a punch,' Daryl agreed. 'You sure you ain't a boy in disguise?'

'Could be,' Jimmy said. 'She sure ain't shaped like a woman. She's missing a couple of essentials.'

I don't know what came over me. It must have been all my worries piling up at once, Bodean and his gun, Flood and Lucy, and the way Ethan was just standing there looking at me with a dark scowl. I hated everybody in sight, so I flew at Jimmy with my fists. He grabbed me around the waist and lifted me off the ground.

'She's a little devil, ain't she?' Jimmy said, twirling me around. I was starting to get dizzy. He dumped me on the ground the way he did before, but I couldn't stop myself, and I came at him again, this time getting a punch in his ribs before he grabbed me up and tossed me to Daryl. Daryl slung me over his shoulder while I pounded on his back with my fists. In the middle of all the laughing and whooping I heard a shout from Ethan. He said, 'Y'all cut it out.'

'Well, what do you think?' Daryl said, tightening his grip around me. 'Looks like Ethan's smitten.'

I caught an upside-down glimpse of Ethan. He was red in the face, either from anger or embarrassment.

'Y'all leave her alone now,' he insisted.

But Daryl just kept spinning me around till I thought I was bound to throw up. Then I suddenly heard another angry voice.

'Is there a problem here?' it said. The world stopped spinning. Daryl lowered me carefully to the ground, and when I got my bearings I saw Flood standing over me. He was glaring at the Grogans.

'No problem,' Daryl said, looking at the ground.

Flood said, 'If I catch you messing with my sister again I'll make you sorry you were ever born.'

'Aw, Flood, we was just having a little fun.'

'Anyhow, she started it,' Jimmy spoke up.

Flood walked toward him till their faces were only inches apart.

'I don't care how it started. I'm just telling you how it's gonna end.'

Jimmy looked down and kicked at the dirt. Flood lingered there a second, then walked over to me and put his hand on my shoulder.

150

'Anybody touches this girl's gonna have to answer to me,' he said.

The Grogans looked away. I could tell they weren't real excited about answering to Flood. Without saying anything else, he walked away.

'I ain't scared of him,' Jimmy said, but his face had turned ash white.

'You all right?' Ethan asked me, his eyes skirting mine.

'What do you care?'

'I was just curious.'

'I'll live,' I said with a shrug.

Then I went off in search of Bodean. It was starting to get dark.

I made a few circles around the church before I found him. He was sitting over behind a big oak tree, and I could barely see him in the shadows. He was clutching his rifle, leaning his face against the barrel. As I got closer, I could hear little whimpering sounds.

'Bodean,' I said softly, bending down next to him. He raised his face to me. It was streaked with dirty tears.

'I didn't mean it,' he said.

'Mean what?'

'It was an accident.'

'What was?' But as soon as I asked, I spotted a little bird lying on the ground a few feet away from us. I moved over to inspect it. It was just a little sparrow. He was about as dead as a bird could be. It made my stomach feel queasy, that tiny thing lying in a lifeless ball on the ground.

'Bodean, you've got no business shooting harmless little birds. A grouse is one thing but this . . .'

'I didn't mean to,' he whimpered. 'It just happened.'

I sat down and put my arm around him. He didn't resist. In fact, he laid his head on my shoulder and started to cry harder.

'I'm bad and mean. I'm gonna bust hell wide open.'

'No, you're not. That's just something I said when I was mad.'

'I didn't want to kill him. I thought I'd just scare him a little.'

'Well, you know what happens when you aim a gun at a bird and pull the trigger. You've shot grouse before.'

He shook his head, wiping his cheeks with the back of his hand. 'I ain't never shot nothing. That was something I made up. I ain't never shot a thing.'

'Yes, you did. I saw those grouse. Flood showed them to me.'

'Daddy just told everybody that. I couldn't shoot nothing when he took me out. I was too scared.'

'Oh,' I said, smoothing back his hair. For some reason that made me feel better about Flood. For all his teasing, he really wanted to protect Bodean, the way he wanted to protect me from the Grogans. In that moment I almost forgave him for hiding the letters. Maybe that was his idea of protecting Bodean, too.

Bodean said, 'I'm never gonna shoot anything else as long as I live.'

'Not even a deer?' I asked, hugging him.

'Not nothing,' he answered, starting to sob. I patted him on the back till his breath returned.

I helped him up, and we started back toward the crowd on the lawn. He held my hand tightly. I looked over my shoulder and saw his BB gun lying there in the grass, lonely and discarded.

'I bet they've got ice cream sandwiches somewhere,' I said, squeezing his hand.

'I ain't hungry.' He sniffed. 'But I reckon I'll split one with you.'

Nineteen

Papa, Bodean, and I went to the bus station to see Norma off. Aunt Macy stayed behind, saying she had some cleaning to do. But I knew the real reason. Aunt Macy can't stand good-byes.

We were all squished in the front seat of the truck, and Bodean had to sit on my lap. He was sulky, and his face was drooping. He felt as heavy and lifeless as a sack of cornmeal.

Norma stared straight ahead with a blank expression, and Papa was whistling the tunes to the country songs on the radio, acting like he was familiar with them all. I knew he wasn't since he almost never turned the radio on. It was as if he just needed something to fill up the silence.

I let my chin rest on Bodean's head and counted the trees as they passed by. It made me think of the way Bodean and I used to count cows on car trips, seeing who could get the most and having to bury them and start over when we passed a graveyard. I wondered if he remembered that game, but I didn't feel it was the time to bring it up.

As we drove through town, I looked at all the familiar sights – the dime store and the diner and the pool hall – and I wondered what it would feel like to leave all those places behind. I didn't think those were the things that I would miss. Not the individual places because surely every town had them. It was more the whole picture – the way Gladys at the drugstore knew me and would let me charge things to Papa, and the way there was always the chance that someone I knew from school would be hanging out on the courthouse steps. It wasn't the greatest town on earth by any means, but at least I had a place in it.

Then there was Ethan. The idea of never seeing him again made my stomach feel exactly the way it did when I had the flu. I couldn't even think about it for very long without wanting to lie down. So I went back to counting trees as if it was very important to know just how many there were between home and the bus station.

'You will write to me, won't you, Dutch?' Norma asked suddenly.

It jarred me so that I jumped a little, and Bodean squirmed in protest.

'I guess so,' I answered. It had never occurred to me that she'd want to hear from me. But she smiled gratefully, or so it seemed, before turning her head away again.

We finally pulled up at the Exxon gas station at the edge of town. That was where the bus stopped to pick up passengers . . . and let them off if that was necessary, but there were always more folks leaving than coming. When we got there the only other person waiting for the bus was a lady, sitting on her suitcase and flipping through a magazine. I recognized her as a cashier at the dime store.

She lifted her eyes lazily to us as we drove up, then looked back down at the glossy pages.

'Afternoon,' Papa said to her as we climbed out of the truck. 'That bus on time?'

She sighed and shook her head. 'Hard to say. Sometimes it is, sometimes it ain't.'

'Can't trust those buses, can you?' Papa said with a chuckle.

'No, sir. Can't never tell. I take this bus every other week down to Norfolk. My boyfriend's there, in the Navy.' She stopped abruptly, as if she had told us too much about herself.

Papa said, 'We better go check in, Norma. They'll want to see your ticket.'

Norma nodded and followed Papa toward the station. Bodean lingered on the blacktop, as if he didn't know what to do with himself.

'Can I have me a Coke?' he called after Papa. Papa paused to count out some change. Bodean couldn't pass a vending machine without getting something out of it. We had a refrigerator full of Cokes at home; but they didn't seem to excite him as much. He snatched the money out of Papa's hands and ran off. Then I was left alone with the lady.

'You work in the dime store, don't you?' I asked.

'I'm the head cashier.'

'I shop there sometimes.'

'Yeah, I've seen you around.'

'Do you like Norfolk?'

She shook her head. 'I ain't much of a city person.'

'What's it like?'

She shrugged. 'Too many folks in too little space. And more cars than you seen in your life. Take you an hour to go five miles. Don't seem like God meant for folks to have that many cars.'

She paused and fanned herself with her magazine. Then she said, 'I'd just as soon stay around here, but my boyfriend's there, see. He's got two more years in the Navy before we can get married. 'Cause I told him a million times if I told him once, I don't wanna be moving all over the place. I told him not to join the Navy, but that man came around school signing everybody up, and he just lost his head. Now he's sorry. I just pray there won't be no war anytime soon.'

I nodded, wanting to get back to the discussion of Norfolk, but her mind had moved on.

'You want to sit down?' she asked. She slid over so I could share her suitcase. I could feel it sagging beneath my weight, but she didn't seem to mind.

'It don't seem right to me,' she went on. 'Somebody coming around telling a bunch of kids to sign up for the Navy. What do they know? That man says I'll give you a lot of money, and you won't never have to worry about it again. What's a kid gonna say? No thank you, I reckon I'll sit here and starve?'

'No, I guess not,' I agreed.

'No, sir. Meantime, what they don't tell you is when the

war come, you the first to go. Walter, that's my boyfriend, he says, "Aw, sugar, there ain't gonna be no war." I say, "How do you figure that? You think folks know when a war's coming? And that man, he'll tell you anything you want to hear just to get you to sign that paper." '

'That's terrible.'

'Isn't it? But then Walter looks around and says, "Well, there ain't nothing for me to do here." Which I can't argue with him about, not the way things are.'

'It's bad everywhere,' I agreed. I didn't want her to think that she and Walter were alone in their problems.

'Still, I say, there ain't much worse than getting your head blown off.'

'What did he say?'

'Aw, he laughed. He thinks I'm just a natural-born worrywart.'

'But he's going to get out of the Navy?'

'Says he is. I don't know. I just don't know.'

There was a moment of silence, then she said, 'You going somewhere?'

'No, I'm just seeing my cousin off. She lives in Richmond.'

She nodded and said, 'Sometimes I ask myself, am I doing the right thing? Should I leave Walter all alone down there? Maybe I should just go ahead and marry him, see what happens. But I feel like I belong here. And when you get away from where you belong, seems like you just go crazy.'

'Yeah.'

159

'But love, it'll do real funny things to you. That's a fact.'

'I know what you mean.'

She looked at me. 'How old are you?'

'Fourteen.'

'That's a good age to be. Seems like you can have the whole world at that age.'

'But you can't really.'

'Naw, nobody can.'

She looked down at her fingers, which were long and slim and very pretty. She wore a small engagement ring on her left hand.

I was about to ask her more about her boyfriend when Bodean ran up, clutching his Coke. He stared at us, then wrapped his lips around his bottle.

'That's my nephew, Bodean,' I said.

'Hey, Bodean. I'm Clareese.'

'I ain't her nephew,' Bodean objected.

'He is, too,' I told her, afraid she would think I was lying. But she just laughed.

'They get real ornery about that age,' she assured me.

Papa and Norma walked up about the same time the bus was pulling up. It came to a wheezing stop in front of us. I stood and let the woman pick up her suitcase. She gave me a sad look, as if we were old friends and she hated to leave me.

'See y'all around sometime,' she said and edged toward the bus, lugging her suitcase with both hands.

It felt strange to think I might never know how her life

turned out, whatever became of her and Walter. It made me see how the world was like one big revolving door . . . different people moving in and touching you briefly before moving out again. It was surprising how fast you could get to know someone just sitting on a suitcase and talking to them.

Norma gave Papa a long hug around his neck. Bodean was hiding behind his Coke bottle, waiting for his turn. But when it came, he backed away from Norma a little, like he was afraid.

'I'm gonna miss you, Bodean,' she said. He beamed and blushed. Next thing I knew he was throwing his arms around her waist. He'd never done that to me, at least not for a long time.

After his hug Bodean looked embarrassed, and he moved over next to Papa and stood close to his leg. Norma turned to me.

She just said, 'Dutch.'

I hugged her stiffly. She hugged back, hard, and kissed me on the cheek. I could smell her perfume, sweet and strong, like magnolia blossoms. For the rest of my life that smell would remind me of her.

'I wish I was more like you,' she said next to my ear.

I drew back and looked at her, not bothering to hide my surprise.

'Why?'

She shrugged. 'I just do. And I wish we could have met a long time ago . . . when we were little, maybe.

161

Before all this crazy stuff started happening.'

I didn't ask what crazy stuff she meant. I felt like I knew. Then a strange thing happened. As I stared at her, I felt as though I was seeing someone completely different, a whole new person. Standing in front of that big bus, she looked small and a little bit scared. And it suddenly occurred to me . . . she's scared, too. She's just like me, and Clareese, and Bodean. Everybody's scared.

In that second a whole world of things became clear to me. I suddenly knew what Papa meant when he said that people weren't all good or all bad – the hard part was knowing that we were a little bit of both. The truth of it struck me so hard that I started to shiver. I had to hug my elbows to keep myself still.

Norma turned away then and started climbing the steps of the bus. She stopped on the top one and looked back.

'Come and see me now, won't you?' she said with a calm smile. 'I'll show you all around the city. There's no end of things for us to do. I'll be real disappointed if you don't come for a visit.'

'I'll come if I can,' I told her.

She grinned. Then the bus doors closed, and she was gone.

'Dutch, honey, what's wrong?' Papa asked.

Without knowing it I had started crying. I sucked in a jagged breath.

'Papa, it's awful,' I said, sniffing hard. 'I really like Norma.'

'Well, there's nothing awful about that.'

'But I didn't know. I didn't know it till just now.'

The three of us stood on the blacktop and watched as the bus pulled off down the road, leaving behind a trail of black exhaust fumes. The chrome glistened under the hot sun. I kept watching until it looked like a little tin can rolling slowly toward the horizon.

Twenty

Bodean was a chatterbox on the way home. He always talked too much when he wanted to pretend something wasn't bothering him. Papa smiled knowingly at me as Bodean rattled on.

'When I grow up, I'm getting out of this place just as soon as I can. I'm leaving here, and y'all won't never see me again. 'Cept to read about me in the newspaper.'

'You're gonna be famous, are you?' Papa asked.

'Yes, sir. I'll be the richest man in the Yew Nited States.'

'Where you gonna get all that money from?' I asked, playing along.

He thought about it, then said, 'I'm gonna invent something. I don't know what yet, but it'll be big. And y'all are gonna come running to me and ask me for money, and maybe I'll give you some, maybe I won't.'

'Where are you gonna live?' I asked.

'Dallas, Texas.'

'Won't you get lonely so far away from home?' Papa asked. 'You don't know anybody in Texas.'

Again Bodean thought. 'I reckon I'll get me a dog.

Papa stopped at the grocery store to get some hamburger for supper. As we climbed out of the truck, I saw Kenny and Ethan playing pinball at the machine out front. Bodean immediately darted in that direction, so I had to follow him. Kenny was engrossed in the game but Ethan nodded at me and mumbled hello. Bodean stood on his tiptoes and leaned over the machine.

'Aw, that don't look so hard,' Bodean said. 'Lemma have a try.'

'You're too little,' Kenny said. He lost his ball about that time and pounded on the glass with his fist.

'I wanna try!' Bodean insisted.

'Don't be a pest, now,' I warned him.

'He can have my turn,' Ethan said. 'Can't do no worse than I'm doing.'

Bodean could barely see what he was doing, but he took it very seriously, sticking his tongue out the side of his mouth while he flipped the handles. When he lost his ball, he punched the machine the way Kenny did.

'Norma's gone, I reckon,' Kenny said to me, returning to the machine.

'Just left.'

He nodded and said, 'She was all right.'

'All right?' Ethan laughed. 'You haven't talked about nothing else since you laid eyes on her.'

'Well, it don't matter now. She's gone, and I don't guess she'll get back here much,' Kenny said.

'Yes, she will!' Bodean assured him. 'She's gonna come

back real soon for a visit. She promised.'

Kenny and Ethan looked at him and started laughing.

'Sounds to me like Kenny's not the only one in love,' Ethan said. 'Is she your sweetheart, Bodean?'

'Do me a favor,' Bodean objected, turning red in the face. 'She's just an old girl.'

'I didn't realize I had so much competition,' Kenny teased, and Bodean's face got even redder.

'Bodean gave her a big hug at the bus station,' I said, going along. 'For two cents he would have got on that bus with her.'

The boys chuckled, and Bodean looked like he might bust a blood vessel. He turned to Ethan and said, 'You're Dutch's sweetheart, ain't you?'

Now it was my turn to blush. My cheeks burned like hot coals.

'Yes, sir,' Bodean went on. 'She's crazy in love with you. She don't talk about nothing else.'

'Bodean . . .' I said weakly.

'Norma would tell you if she was here. That's the whole reason Dutch put on all that makeup. She thought you was gonna drop dead. She said . . .'

'Shut up, Bodean,' I hissed.

'I ain't told a lie,' Bodean said, jutting out his jaw.

Kenny and Ethan didn't say anything. Ethan's face was perfectly still and clueless. I couldn't even guess what he was thinking, but I wasn't sure I wanted to know.

Papa came out then with a bag of groceries, and I was

never so happy to see a person. I grabbed Bodean's arm and headed in his direction.

'Afternoon, boys,' Papa said. They nodded at him.

Once inside the truck I put my face in my hands and took a deep breath.

'What's wrong with you?' Papa asked.

'Nothing. The heat, I reckon.'

'She's in love,' Bodean said.

Papa just smiled and started up the truck.

All the way home I tried to figure out some way of never seeing Ethan again. Maybe I could avoid him all summer, but things would get tricky when school started. I couldn't get mad at Bodean, even if he was sitting there with a smug grin on his face. You can't go around telling other people's secrets when you've got some of your own.

My head was still reeling when we pulled up in the driveway. I hardly noticed a strange car sitting there, parked beside the Chevrolet. This car was blue, an old Toyota.

'Looks like we got company,' Papa said.

Bodean and I both hurried toward the house, eager to see who the visitor was. Aunt Macy met us at the door. She was wringing her hands.

'I thought y'all would never get here.'

'Who is it?' I asked in a low voice.

'You better go see for yourself.'

We came barreling into the den, near about knocking each other over. The visitor was sitting on the couch. Flood stood next to the window, staring out.

She looked just the way I remembered. Black hair cut in soft curls around her face. Eyes as black as the night sky. Her cheeks were pink, her mouth full and red. And when she smiled, there was a tiny gap between her front teeth. There was a fine spray of freckles across her nose, just like there was on Bodean's. She smiled at us and tugged nervously at her earlobe.

Flood said, 'Bodean, this here's your mama.'

Bodean blinked at her. He looked at me, then at Flood, and finally back at Becky. His bottom lip was trembling.

'You ain't my mama,' Bodean said.

Becky's smile flickered a little. 'I didn't think you'd remember me.'

'I don't remember you 'cause you ain't my mama.'

'Bodean,' I said quietly.

'My mama's no good!' Bodean announced, and with that he turned and took off up the stairs. We all stayed quiet. Flood turned his head back toward the window.

The door slammed and Papa came in. He stood still in his tracks, looking at Becky.

'Lord above,' he said.

He put the groceries down and went over to her. She stood slowly, and he put his arms around her, patting her softly on the back. Becky started sniffling.

'It's about time something good happened around here,' Papa said, standing back and holding her by the shoulders.

She looked down. 'I'm not back to stay, Papa Earl.'

'Well, it's a joy to see your face.'

They smiled at each other a few seconds, and then she turned to me.

'You remember me, don't you, Dutch?'

I nodded dumbly. She stretched out an arm, and we hugged awkwardly, limbs and chins bumping. She was skinnier than I remembered.

'Well, I'm not sure I would have known *you*. You're all grown up,' she said, smoothing back my hair.

The room got quiet. You could almost hear everyone breathing. Finally Papa picked up the grocery bag, and it rustled loudly in the silence.

'You can stay for dinner at least, can't you?' Papa asked.

'I think so. I mean, if it's no trouble.'

' 'Course it's no trouble. I just wish we'd got something a little fancier than hamburger.' Turning to me, he said, 'But maybe Dutch can find a way to dress it up.'

That was the cue for us to leave. We walked out together, and I couldn't help noticing the look on Flood's face as we left. He watched us, his eyes pleading a little, like he was afraid of what lay in store. Then he turned back to the window, staring at the trees and the sky and the open field, as if the world was one big mystery to him.

Twenty One

Becky ate supper with us that night, but Flood didn't. His empty place sat there like an ugly scar, and everybody tried to avoid looking at it.

Bodean sat very close to me and stared hard at his plate, even though he didn't eat much of his food. Once or twice I saw Becky inspecting him with her head slightly cocked, as if trying to see some of herself in him. I knew she'd have to look pretty hard to see that. The only thing he got from her was her freckles and maybe the shape of her nose. Everything else was pure Flood.

Aunt Macy and Papa did most of the talking, asking Becky all about Norfolk and what she'd been doing with herself. She said she lived in an apartment, and for a long time she worked in a real estate office as a secretary. Finally she had taken the exam herself and passed, so she was a full-fledged real estate agent.

Papa said, 'I can't hardly picture you as a business woman.'

'It doesn't feel much like business,' she said with that light laugh I remembered so well. 'It's more like house-hunting. I always say I wouldn't try to sell somebody a house I wouldn't own myself. I can't afford a house right now, so it's sort of a vicarious pleasure.'

Papa smiled and I did, too. I made a mental note to look up the word 'vicarious.'

'You get on all right by yourself then,' Papa said.

'Breaking even,' she said.

'No, I mean . . . in a city that size. I hear the crime rate is pretty high there.'

'Oh, it's all right if you stay out of the bad areas. You can't go walking at night by yourself or anything. But other than that, you do as you please.'

'Do you have any friends there?' asked Aunt Macy. I sensed she wanted to know if Becky had a boyfriend. I was curious myself.

'A few. Mostly girls from work. I'm in a bowling league.'

'You always were the best bowler I ever saw for a woman,' Papa said.

Aunt Macy told her about our visit from Norma.

'Oh, yes. Dutch told me,' Becky said, and I dropped my fork with a clink.

I could feel my heart thumping as everybody looked at me. My eyes connected with Becky's, and she gave me a reassuring smile.

'She did?' Aunt Macy asked.

'Yes. Right before supper . . . she mentioned it, but we didn't get around to details.'

I let out a slow sigh of relief as Aunt Macy described Norma and talked about how much we all enjoyed her visit. Then they went on to discuss Uncle Eugene, and Becky was surprised to hear that he and Aunt Fran were getting a divorce.

'I always wanted to meet Uncle Eugene,' Becky said. 'I have a soft spot in my heart for the black sheep of the family. I was one myself, you know. My folks didn't like the idea of me marrying Flood. Being as young as I was and all.'

The mention of Flood's name made everyone turn quiet and still.

'Can I be excused?' Bodean asked. He almost never did that. He usually just darted away from the table whenever the spirit moved him.

'You haven't touched your black-eyed peas,' said Aunt Macy.

'I don't want 'em. They make me puke.'

Aunt Macy sighed and looked to Becky. Becky seemed confused about the whole situation. She finally glanced over at Bodean, and they stared at each other for a moment without speaking.

'Run on, then,' said Aunt Macy.

Bodean jumped up and hurried out of the kitchen. We sat and listened to his footsteps pounding up the stairs. The door to his room slammed with a thud.

Becky cleared her throat. 'It's funny. I was thinking I should tell him to eat his vegetables. That's what a mother should do. But I just didn't feel like I had the right. I mean . . . ' She hesitated, sucking in a breath. '. . . I don't even know what foods he likes.'

We just looked at her, all of us as nervous as if someone had just dropped dead at the table.

'He don't like much,' Aunt Macy finally said. 'Nothing but junk, anyhow.'

'Well, I guess it's the age,' said Becky.

We all nodded at once, eager to agree with her.

Papa said, 'He'll come around, sweetheart. He's just a little confused.'

'Oh, I know. I knew it would be this way. All the way driving down here I kept saying to myself, "Now, don't expect too much."'

She stopped again, this time pressing her knuckles to her lips. Her face had turned pink, and her lashes fluttered hard.

'I guess I've been wondering,' Papa said slowly, 'and mind you, you don't have to answer this if you don't want to . . . but what made you decide to come back here after all this time?'

She swallowed and looked up at him. 'I just think there comes a time when you've got to clean out your life, just like you clean out your closets. And it seemed to me that time had come.'

Papa nodded, as if he liked that answer. I liked it, too. And I liked Becky. She was much as I remembered, but something about her had changed. She talked more, and the things she said sounded wise. A lot of her shyness was gone, and in its place was confidence and grace. Something she must have picked up in the city, I decided. And then I knew that the world didn't have to make people worse; sometimes it made them better.

After supper Papa went up and had a talk with Bodean. I don't know what he said, but he soon came down with Bodean in tow. Papa was smiling, but Bodean looked like he might burst into tears.

Becky and I were drying the last of the supper dishes, and we stopped and looked at them. Without saying a word, Bodean went over and stood beside Becky, staring hard at his tennis shoes.

'Do you want to go for a walk with me?' Becky asked.

'No,' said Bodean. 'But Grandpa says I have to.'

Becky bent down and tried to look at him, but he turned away.

'You don't have to if you don't want to.'

Bodean shrugged. 'I ain't got nothing better to do.'

I stood at the kitchen window and watched them walking toward the tobacco barn. They were holding hands. The sky was turning pink as the sun went down. In the soft light the tobacco leaves looked almost healthy, blooming all around them like giant gold flowers. It looked like a painting I had seen somewhere.

Twenty Two

Bodean didn't say a word about his walk when he got back. He went straight to his room and stayed there. Around eleven o'clock he came knocking on my door. I was having another try at starting a journal, and this effort wasn't going much better than the others. I had only written one sentence: 'Becky came back today, like I always knew she would.' I couldn't write anymore; I just wanted to stare at the way those words looked. When the knock came I quickly stashed the notebook under my pillow. I didn't want Bodean to even know such a thing existed.

He came in wearing his pajamas and scratching his head. He was all bleary-eyed.

'Can I sleep in your room?'

'What for?'

'I keep having bad dreams.'

'Sure, go ahead.'

He crawled into the extra bed and lay there staring at the ceiling.

'What were your dreams about?'

'That bird I shot. He came back to get me. Only he kept getting bigger and bigger.' He paused, then turned to me.

'Do you think things come back from the dead?'

'No. Not birds, anyhow.'

That seemed to make him relax. I was trying to think of a way to ask him something about Becky when I heard loud voices rising up from downstairs. It sounded like Flood. Bodean looked at me with big eyes.

I got out of bed and went to the door.

'Can I come with you?' he asked.

'No, you better not.'

He did anyway. He followed me all the way downstairs. We stopped on the bottom step and peeked into the kitchen. Flood and Becky were there. She was sitting at the table, and he was pacing the floor. His face was red, and he looked very upset. I couldn't tell if he was drunk or not.

'Go back upstairs,' I whispered to Bodean.

'Why?'

'Because this looks personal.'

'If you get to listen, I do, too.'

It was hard to argue with that. In a way he had more of a right to listen than I did, but I didn't want him to take up my bad habit of eavesdropping. I couldn't help feeling that Bodean was too young to know the kind of secrets you pick up from listening in doorways.

'Go on, now. I mean it.'

He gave me a hard look, then turned and went upstairs. I settled down on the bottom step and waited.

Flood said, 'I don't know who you think you are. You just waltz in here after six years, expecting to be his mother.

Well, you're not his mother anymore. You gave that up, remember?'

'You can't give up something like that,' Becky said quietly.

'You ain't taking my boy off, and that's that.'

'I don't want him forever, Flood. I'd just like to spend some time with him.'

'If you'd stayed here you could have spent all the time you wanted with him.'

'I couldn't stay here. You know that.'

'Why the hell not!' he snapped, turning on her. 'Okay, so you didn't want to live with me. But what kind of mother goes off and leaves her son?'

'The kind who's too young to have a son in the first place. The kind who's too confused to know what she's doing. Flood, I was only a baby when he was born. I was nineteen! Do you think I had any idea how to be a mother?'

'No, that's my point. You didn't then and you don't now.'

'You never did understand,' she said, shaking her head slowly. 'You just didn't see what was happening around you. You thought you could just marry somebody and stick them away like a piece of furniture. You never listened . . . you never saw what was happening to me.'

'I saw enough. I saw you running around with everything in pants. And I sure as hell heard you say you were leaving me for Calvin Reynolds.'

Becky's face turned pale. She looked down at her fingers.

'That wasn't anything, Flood. That was over before it began.'

'But you left here with him. You must have thought it was something.'

'I guess I did at the time.'

There was a long silence. I was starting to think they wouldn't speak again.

Then Becky said, 'It was your idea to have a baby. And I thought, maybe so. Maybe it's a good idea. Anything to get you interested in me again. Maybe it would be something for us to talk about. Something we could share. But that didn't happen. It just made you more distant. Like you were mad at me for giving you one more thing to tie you down. You even said that to me once. Remember?'

Flood turned his back on her, leaning against the wall with his arms crossed.

'Can't you understand how lost I was?' she said in a near whisper.

'What about me?'

'We're not talking about you!' she shouted, slamming her hand down on the table. 'Dammit, Flood, for once in my life I'm going to make you think about me.'

He didn't answer. She lifted her hand to her lips, then started rubbing it on her jeans.

'I felt so tired all the time. I could hardly get out of bed in the morning. I didn't have the energy to get dressed or cook or go for a walk. By six o'clock I wanted to crawl in bed and go to sleep. One day I looked in the mirror and I thought, "My God, I'm an old woman!" I was barely out of my teens and I was old. I had a husband who didn't know how to talk to me. I had a baby that I didn't know how to take care of. And when I looked ahead, all I could see was years and years of feeling old and tired. Flood, I just wanted to live.'

He didn't say anything to that. Becky slid her chair back like she might stand up, but she didn't.

'So then Calvin came along, talking to me the way you once did. Telling me all the things I never thought I'd hear again. I just wanted to believe him so much. I wanted to believe someone could be in love with me.'

'I married you, didn't I? Wasn't that enough?'

'No. It wasn't. That's the trouble with you. You keep thinking you can get to a place where you can stop trying and everything will take care of itself. You have to work at keeping things, Flood. Don't you know that?'

Flood turned around to look at her. 'I know it now,' he said.

Becky looked down, as if his words embarrassed her. 'Anyway, all that's over and done with. I know I made a mistake. But that doesn't mean it's too late to correct it.'

'Maybe it is too late.'

She shook her head. 'I think I deserve another chance.' When Flood didn't respond to that, she said, 'At least try to consider what's best for Bodean.'

'That's all I ever considered. That's all I've been considering for the past nine years.'

181

'Is that why you hid my letters?'

I jumped so quickly I was afraid I might have betrayed myself. My heart was pounding so loud it was hard to believe they couldn't hear it.

But Flood fixed his eyes firmly on her. He looked as if he might faint.

'Who told you that?'

'Nobody had to tell me. I know he never got them. For a long time I figured you just told him not to write back to me. That was bad enough. But one day it just occurred to me . . . a boy has to at least be curious about his mother. And I remembered that look on your face the night I walked out of here. You're not the kind of man who forgives. But you're the kind of man who can justify anything.'

Flood looked down at his shoes.

She stood and walked slowly toward him. 'How could you do it? How could you be so cruel? I don't blame you for punishing me. But to punish your own son . . .'

'Keeping you out of his life didn't seem like much of a punishment.'

When Becky raised her hand I thought for sure she was going to hit him. Instead she placed it carefully on his shoulder.

'Let me have him for a little while. Please. I think it would be good for him, too.'

Flood said, 'It would have been better for him if you'd died.'

Becky nodded, biting her lip. 'Maybe so. But I'm not

dead, am I? We can't change that, unless you want to strangle me now and get it over with.'

Flood laughed and looked at her. 'There's been times when that sounded like a real good idea.'

Becky laughed, too, a nervous kind of laugh.

'God, I loved you,' Becky said suddenly, and Flood's smile evaporated. 'I thought if I could wake up beside you every day, I'd never want anything more from life. Maybe that was where I went wrong. I wanted too much from you. I wanted everything.'

The expression on Flood's face was strained and desperate. He looked away. His throat tightened as he swallowed. And then I saw . . . or thought I saw . . . something that would stick in my mind from that day forward. A spot on his cheek glistened in the light. Becky reached up and touched it.

'I couldn't love you the way I wanted to,' Flood said. 'I felt like I was gonna disappear.'

'I know,' Becky answered. It sounded like a secret language.

Flood nodded, then walked away. He grabbed a kitchen chair so hard I thought the wood might crumble under his fingers.

'Damn,' he said: 'If Bodean wants to go with you, he can. I won't try to stop him.'

'Thank you,' Becky said, shutting her eyes. They fluttered open again, and she smiled. 'I always hated that name, Bodean.'

Flood smiled back. 'Why do you think I called him that?'

He turned away then and walked out the back door. Becky stood in the middle of the room waiting, as if she thought he might return. Then she moved on, and all I could see was the light reflecting off the linoleum floor.

When I turned around, I saw Bodean sitting at the top of the stairs. He hadn't missed a word.

Twenty Three

Two weeks later Becky came back to pick up Bodean and take him off to Norfolk. He was going to spend the rest of the summer there. He didn't like the idea at first and kept swearing that he wasn't going to go. Every time Aunt Macy packed his suitcase he unpacked it. When Papa sat him down and tried to tell him about how to behave while he was away from home, he said, 'You're wasting your breath. I ain't going nowhere.' We all just kept ignoring him and continued to make plans.

Flood stayed out of it. He had turned quiet and serious after Becky's visit. He just did his work during the day, and he stopped going out in the evening. He sat in the den, flipping through the newspaper or staring at the walls until bedtime.

I didn't know what to expect the day Becky was due to arrive. I thought we might have to drag Bodean kicking and screaming from his room, but when I came into the kitchen that morning, he was sitting at the table with his suitcase beside him, staring at the clock on the wall.

'Looks like you're going after all,' I said, trying not to make a big deal out of it.

'I don't have nothing better to do.'

Becky showed up right on time. She came inside for a cup of coffee and tried to make conversation with Bodean.

'I hope you don't get carsick,' she said.

'I've been in a car before,' he said, rolling his eyes.

'Yes, I know. But it's an awful long drive.'

'My class went on a field trip to Appomattox last year,' he said. 'And that's a long way away.'

'Did you have a good time?'

'It won't nothing special. Just a dumb old courthouse. We got one of those right here.'

We all laughed. Bodean fought back a grin.

Flood came in from the fields about that time. He nodded at Becky and poured himself a cup of coffee. She watched him walk across the room, but when he turned his head back toward her, she looked away. It seemed like they both wanted to talk to each other but didn't know how. I kept waiting for them to look at each other, to realize they were still in love and couldn't stand to be apart. But that didn't happen.

'He won't eat his vegetables unless you keep after him,' Aunt Macy said to Becky. 'And getting him to bathe is like pulling teeth.'

'Do me a favor,' Bodean said with a huff.

'He sleeps with a night-light,' I added.

'That's a lie!' he snapped.

'Well, he used to.'

'There are some boys in my apartment building about

your age,' Becky told him. 'I always see them throwing a softball in the yard. Do you play softball?'

He shrugged. 'When I get the time.'

'Well, you'll have plenty of time,' Papa said. 'This is a vacation.'

'When can we go?' Bodean asked, squirming.

'Well, now if you want to,' Becky answered.

He stood up, trying to lift his suitcase, which was twice as big as he was. Flood moved over and took it from him.

'Feels like you packed everything you own,' Flood said. 'You planning on staying forever?'

'No,' Bodean said quickly.

Flood smiled.

We all went outside to Becky's car. She opened the trunk, and Flood put the suitcase inside. She helped him move it around so the trunk would close. I stood watching them as they worked. They looked the way a married couple should . . . silently working toward the same goal.

We took turns hugging Bodean. When he got to me, he just passed his arms over me real quick, as though he was afraid of catching something. I didn't take it personally.

'Well, this is it,' Bodean said, sounding like a grownup. I almost laughed. He looked so small and pathetic standing there, his hair all out of place, both knees skinned from some recent adventure. Then he and Becky got in the car. She rolled down the window and said, 'I'll take good care of him.'

'I know that,' Papa said. 'It's you we're worried about.'

We all laughed again. Then the car started up and drove away. I couldn't see much of Bodean's head except his cowlick sticking up like a spray of water.

A strange kind of silence fell around us. Nobody wanted to move. It was almost as if we were afraid to go back to a world without Bodean.

'Well, I got some pickles to make,' said Aunt Macy. She walked back to the house.

Flood took off his hat and scratched his head. He walked in a little circle, stopping to kick at a tuft of grass. Papa put a hand on his arm and said, 'Reckon we ought to get to work, don't you?'

Flood nodded. There wasn't much work to be done, but I knew Papa would find some. Together they walked off toward the field, their legs moving in the same rhythm. From a distance they looked so similar, walking together in perfect time, like images in a mirror.

Later that afternoon Aunt Macy and I went into town and treated ourselves to an ice-cream sundae at the drugstore. Gladys was working behind the counter, and she talked to us while we ate. She'd already heard about Bodean going off to Norfolk with Becky.

'I reckon he'll be too big for his britches when he gets back,' Gladys said.

'He's already too big for his britches,' I said.

'Well, just wait. He'll be worse. My grandchild, Cora's daughter? She went off to cheerleading camp and came back with a face full of makeup and smoking cigarettes. I told

Cora she was asking for trouble letting that child go away so young.'

'You can't protect them from the world,' Aunt Macy said wisely. 'They're gonna see it sooner or later.'

'The later the better, I say,' Gladys replied.

When she walked away, Aunt Macy shook her head and clucked her tongue. 'I don't know why folks have to know everybody's business. Just bored with their own lives, I suppose.'

I didn't feel I had the right to agree, being the terrible eavesdropper that I was.

'Well,' said Aunt Macy with a sigh, 'your brother's gonna have a real time of it now that Bodean's gone. Maybe it'll make him grow up a little. I'd give anything for him to settle down.'

'Oh, he will,' I said, thinking of Becky. 'It's just a matter of time.'

'Maybe,' she agreed. 'He's been so mad at Becky all these years. Never would forgive her for leaving him like that. Maybe now he can get past it. A grudge like that can ruin your life.'

I thought about her grudge against Uncle Eugene and wondered if it had ruined her life. But I knew better than to ask. So I said, 'I don't think Flood ever stopped loving Becky.'

She sighed. 'Well, they were about as in love as I'd ever seen two people when they got married. Always cooing and sighing and staring into each other's eyes. But the truth of it was, they didn't know how to be friends. Couldn't hardly talk when you left them in a room alone. I reckon it was more Flood's fault than it was hers. He didn't ever learn how to get close to people. Even as a boy he was like that. But it's something he's got to figure out if he wants to get on with his life.'

'It's not too late.'

'No. I don't suppose it ever is.'

We didn't talk any more about Flood and Becky. Aunt Macy went on to tell me about her first date with her first husband, Henry. He took her to see a scary movie, and halfway into it he stood up to go to the bathroom and fainted.

'They had to call the ambulance and everything. It scared the life out of me. I thought he was dead! He knocked his head open when he hit the floor, and there was blood every-where. That's how I spent my first date, sitting in the waiting room of a hospital while they stitched up Henry's head!'

She giggled, licking the ice cream off her spoon. 'That's when I fell in love with him. The idea of a big man like that passing out in a scary movie. Well, I never could resist a sensitive man.'

I thought about Ethan and wondered if he was a sensitive man. I wondered, too, if there had ever been a single moment like that when I suddenly realized I was in love with him. Or maybe that moment had yet to come.

'I guess you just know,' I said, thinking out loud. 'I mean, when it happens.'

'Sometimes you do, and sometimes it takes you a while to catch on.' She paused and looked at me. 'Have you got somebody special in mind?'

'Maybe.'

'Well, don't rush it. There'll come a day when love's the only thing on your mind. Use this time to think about other things.'

'What things?' I asked, because I couldn't imagine anything quite as interesting as being in love.

Aunt Macy didn't have an answer for that. She just smiled and counted out the money for our ice cream.

We had a quiet supper that night. I missed the sound of Bodean's voice, whining and complaining about the food or bragging about some accomplishment. When we finished eating everybody went their separate way. Papa read the paper while Aunt Macy and I cleaned up. Flood announced that he was going out for a while. Aunt Macy breathed a heavy sigh when he left. She was probably dreading his return, trying to get him into bed without Papa's seeing his condition.

Papa went to sleep early, and Aunt Macy and I stayed up to watch a movie on TV. We didn't expect to see Flood again till way past midnight, but around ten o'clock we heard voices on the porch. Aunt Macy stiffened and looked at me. I just shrugged. A few minutes later Flood appeared in the living room.

'Y'all still awake?' he asked.

'Just watching TV,' said Aunt Macy.

191

'Mind if we join you?'

She was too surprised to answer, but Flood took that as a yes. He motioned to somebody, and then a woman followed him into the room. It was Lucy Cabbot from church. In the shadowy light she resembled Becky. She had the same dark eyes and dark hair, though Lucy's was longer, and I could tell the curl in it wasn't natural. She was small, like Becky, and smiled the way she did, though her teeth didn't have that tiny gap. Some people might say she was prettier than Becky, but they'd be wrong.

'I guess y'all know Lucy,' Flood said.

'Of course we do,' said Aunt Macy. I just grunted.

'Have a seat,' Flood said to Lucy.

'I hope we're not interrupting,' Lucy said, easing herself down next to me on the couch. I wanted to slide away but thought better of it.

'Oh, it's just a silly old movie,' said Aunt Macy. I couldn't believe how agreeable she was being.

'You want a drink or something?' Flood asked.

'An iced tea would be fine.'

Flood went away and came back with two glasses of tea. I stared dumbly at him, waiting for some kind of explanation. But he just grinned at me as if he didn't have anything to say for himself.

It was quiet except for the television, which had suddenly turned into a jumbled mess of noise. Nobody was paying any attention, even though we all stared at the screen.

'We went bowling,' Flood suddenly announced. 'Lucy beat the pants off of me.'

'You weren't even trying, Flood,' Lucy said. My blood curdled. I couldn't stand to hear her say his name.

'I'm just out of practice is all.'

I gave Lucy a critical look. She seemed overdressed for bowling. Nobody went bowling in nice black pants and a pink angora sweater, not to mention a strand of tiny pearls. She was too skinny anyway, and skinny people are not supposed to wear black. Everyone knows that.

I sat there taking deep breaths and trying to calm myself. It was all I could do to stop myself from exploding at Flood, asking him just what he thought he was doing going out with a woman when his wife had been sitting there in the kitchen that very morning.

'This sure is good tea,' Lucy said.

'Dutch made it. She runs the kitchen around here.'

Lucy smiled at me. It was a pleasant enough smile. She had perfect teeth, and her eyes crinkled nicely. But no matter what, I couldn't bring myself to smile back at her.

'Anybody want to play a game of cards?' Flood asked. 'Gin rummy?'

'Lord, it's been ages since I've played gin rummy,' Aunt Macy said.

That was it for me. I stood up abruptly, jostling Lucy a little bit as I went.

'Where are you off to, Dutch?' Flood asked.

'To bed. I'm tired.'

'Don't you want to play?'

'No, thanks.'

'Good night,' Lucy called after me, but I didn't look back.

As I headed up the stairs, I heard Flood talking in a loud, jolly voice that I hadn't heard him use in years.

'Now, if you want to see a good cardplayer, you ought to try playing with my boy. He's something else, isn't he, Macy?'

'Where is Bodean?' Lucy asked.

'In Norfolk,' Flood said just as calm as you please. 'Visiting with his mama.'

Twenty Four

That wasn't the last we saw of Lucy. She came over the next night for supper, and to my shock, nobody seemed to mind. In fact, Papa and Aunt Macy seemed pleased as punch.

She was shy at first and hardly said anything, but by the time we got to dessert she was telling us her whole life story. She talked so much, in fact, that she hardly ate anything on her plate. No wonder she was so skinny.

She was a piano teacher, and she taught classes at the elementary school as well as individual lessons in her home. Flood made some joke about sending Bodean to her for lessons, and everyone had a good hoot over that.

'I'd love to see that boy sitting at a piano,' said Flood, chuckling away. 'He's all thumbs.'

'Anybody can learn,' she assured him. 'He might even like it. Music is the universal language.'

'Yuck,' I said without meaning to.

'How about you, Dutch?' she had the nerve to say to me. 'Wouldn't you like to learn the piano?'

'I'd rather have my fingernails pulled out.'

'Now, listen to you,' Aunt Macy said. 'You're starting to talk like Bodean.'

I didn't care. I wanted to make Lucy mad. I wanted her to hate me so much that she'd never set foot in our house again.

But that didn't work. The very next day she came home with Flood after church for Sunday lunch. I could hardly look at her during the meal, even though she kept trying to talk to me. She said she was starting a youth choir at church and wondered if I'd be interested.

'I'm not much of a singer,' I answered.

'That doesn't matter. You'll catch on.'

'Why not, Dutch?' Papa said. 'You don't have much to keep you busy now that Bodean's gone.'

'I've got plenty of things to do.'

The subject was dropped then, but I could feel Papa staring at me, wondering what was wrong.

After lunch Lucy helped me wash the dishes, even though I told her not to. She kept on trying to talk to me, and it was getting harder and harder to ignore her. She was the cheery type. It didn't seem you could do anything to make her mad.

Finally she said, 'Dutch, I get the feeling you don't like me.'

I looked at her. Her hair was shining in the sunlight. She had on a little makeup, which made her eyes look bigger and her cheeks look pinker. She was pretty; I had to give her that. But she wasn't Becky.

Suddenly a thought occurred to me, something I really should have seen before. It was no coincidence that Flood went out and found another woman, right when Becky had come back into his life. I thought of Norma telling me to flirt with Kenny to make Ethan jealous. That was an old trick that everybody used, she said, and now Flood was using it, too. He was trying to make Becky jealous. The minute I realized that, everything came together and I felt better. I even smiled.

'I don't have anything against you,' I said.

She smiled back. 'Good. Because I was hoping we could be friends.'

'Okay,' I said. I knew she wouldn't be around long enough for me to make good on that promise.

The only thing that worried me was the way Flood acted even after Lucy had gone. He kept on smiling and whistling, as if he didn't have a care in the world. He didn't complain about the weather or try to pick fights with Papa. He didn't even try to aggravate Aunt Macy. His happy mood didn't fit in with the plan. When Lucy wasn't around, he should have gone back to being his grumpy self. That annoyed me, and I wanted to tell him to drop the act. I was on to him.

Papa could tell I was upset about something. That night, out of the blue, he asked me if I wanted to play a game of Chinese checkers. That was something we hadn't done since I was little. It used to be my favorite game. When he suggested it I gave in, mainly because I was tired of sitting around moping. But I wasn't really in the mood for games, and it showed in the way I played. I could usually beat him, but right away I fell behind and couldn't figure out how to catch up.

He studied the board as he puffed his pipe. He only smoked his pipe occasionally, usually when he was playing a game like that. I liked to look at him, biting down on the stem and pausing now and then to let out a stream of gray-blue smoke. It made him look smart, like a college professor, and I liked the way it smelled.

'What's wrong with you, Dutch?' he finally said. 'I believe you're letting me win.'

'I don't know. I guess I can't concentrate.'

'Got something on your mind?'

'Maybe.'

He nodded, still puffing his pipe. 'Something to do with Flood's new girlfriend?'

I frowned. 'Don't say that. She's not his girlfriend.'

He laughed quietly. 'Well, it sure looks that way to me.'

'He's just using her,' I said, sounding out my theory, 'to make Becky jealous.'

'Is that so?'

'Yes. And I think the whole thing is stupid.' I paused, then added, 'I think somebody ought to warn that girl. I feel sorry for her, if you want to know the truth.'

'Why's that?'

'Because he's not interested in her. I told you, it's just a trick.'

'Well, I think maybe that's Flood's business, don't you?'

'No. It's everybody's. I mean, maybe this trick will work,

but what if it doesn't? He's got to move fast if he wants to save his marriage.'

Papa put his pipe down and leaned across the table. 'Honey, Flood's not married anymore.'

'But Becky is Bodean's mama!'

'That's right, she is. And she always will be. But that don't mean she has to be Flood's wife.'

'You don't understand,' I complained, pushing the checker game away from me. I had lost what little interest I had.

'I believe I do. You want Becky and Flood back together. I can understand that. We'd all like that. But I just don't think it's fair for us to meddle in Flood's business that way.'

'It's our business, too. It's our family.'

Papa stared at me for a minute, then rubbed his chin. I couldn't figure out why he was smiling.

'Don't you want Flood to be happy?' he asked.

'Yes, but . . . you're the one who said families ought to stay together. You're the one who's always telling me that.'

'Yes, I know. And I believe it. But sometimes, no matter how much you believe something or want something, it doesn't turn out that way.'

'This one's going to turn out fine. I know it is.'

He studied me, running the stem of his pipe across his lips. I could tell something about my attitude bothered him. I didn't know exactly what, and I wasn't sure he did, either.

The back door slammed, and Flood came walking into the kitchen. To my relief he was alone. What was even better, he wasn't whistling or smiling. He had a serious expression on his face. I stared at him hopefully, but his eyes didn't meet mine. He was looking at Papa.

'Evening,' Papa said. 'Your sister's handing this game to me on a silver platter.'

Flood nodded, as though he wasn't real concerned about it.

'Can I talk to you for a minute?' he asked.

'Sure. Have a seat.'

I stood up, figuring this was a grown-up discussion. But Flood put his hand on my shoulder.

'You can stay if you want to.'

I was so shocked that I didn't know what to say. It was peculiar having Flood talk to me like that, in a real adult way, as if I were an equal. I just lowered myself back into my seat, staring at him.

Flood stayed standing and kept his eyes fixed on the table. He looked a little bit afraid.

'I've been thinking about the farm,' he said.

Papa nodded. 'I reckon we all have.'

'Yeah, well. I want to do something about it.'

Papa ran his pipe across his teeth. It made a clicking sound. Flood finally pulled out a chair and sat down.

'There's something I've been keeping from you.' He swallowed and looked up at Papa. 'I've been putting some money away. Little bit here and there. I sold my old stamp collection a while back. Been winning some money off of pool now and again.' He laughed nervously. 'And every time you gave me my pay I stuck some of it in a savings account. It all kind of added up over the years.'

'That was a very wise thing to do,' Papa said.

'Yeah, well.' Flood paused and scratched his head. 'The thing is I was planning on using it to get out of here. I was gonna just take off out west . . . me and Bodean . . . set up that cattle ranch I've always talked about. I been planning that for years, and what's more, I wasn't even going to tell you about it. I was just gonna up and go.'

I looked at Papa to see how he was taking this. His expression was completely calm, as if none of it surprised him.

'Anyhow,' Flood said with a sigh, 'that's just not gonna happen. I'm stuck here, and that's just how it is.'

'You're free to go anytime. Always have been.'

'Oh, I know. I didn't mean it like that. What I mean is . . . hell, I never been any good with talking.'

He laughed a little. Papa smiled.

'The thing is,' he went on after taking a breath, 'I kept on thinking I was better than this. Like I somehow deserved more. But lately I've been looking around, and it seems to me this isn't so bad. There's some things you just can't leave behind, no matter how much you think you want to. I mean, my boy was born here. This is what he knows. It's not fair to uproot him from all that.'

Papa nodded, puffing on his pipe.

'And besides, I reckon I ought to keep him close to his mama. They've got some catching up to do.'

'Well,' Papa said, 'you've got yourself to think about, too.'

'I know that. Believe me, I think about myself plenty. Too much, I reckon.' He looked down at his fingers. They had been scrubbed clean, and his fingernails were short and almost bleached white. 'The thing is, lately I've been finding my own reasons for staying around.'

'I thought you probably had,' Papa said.

Flood struggled with a smile, trying to fight it back, but it just kept on coming. Then he reached into his pocket and handed Papa a thick white envelope.

'There's fifteen thousand dollars in there. It's everything I've got.'

'That's a pretty hefty sum,' Papa said, weighing the envelope in his palm.

'Well, not enough to make a dent in our loan. I know that. But I figure it might buy us some time. It'll make a decent payment on that tractor, anyhow.'

'That it will,' Papa agreed.

'And I reckon after that we'll just see what happens. Like you said, we've pulled ourselves out of messes before.'

'Yep. Bigger messes than this, too.'

'Not much bigger, though.'

Papa laughed. 'No, not much.'

They chuckled together. I couldn't quite see the humor.

After their laughter dribbled away Flood shook his head and let out a sigh. 'I just never wanted to work through a problem. Never figured out how, I guess. I kept thinking if

I ignored something, it would go away. And that's the truth, too. Becky went, and now the farm's going . . .'

'It doesn't have to be that way,' Papa said.

'Well, that's what I figured out. Becky says you got to work at keeping things. She's right about that. That's a pretty big lesson to learn at my age.'

Having said that, he pushed his chair back and stood up, stuffing his hands in his back pockets.

'So, that's all I've got to say.'

He edged away. Papa looked up.

'This is a real good thing you've done,' he said.

Flood shrugged. 'Well . . .'

He hesitated for a second, then walked toward the back door. But when he got there, he stopped and looked at Papa again.

'I still think that tractor's a piece of junk,' he said, sounding like the old Flood.

But Papa just smiled. 'I think you're probably right.'

Flood went out, and the door creaked shut. Papa sat there for a long moment staring at the space where Flood had been. Then he turned to me, his lips twitching.

'I believe it's your move,' he said.

Twenty Five

The next afternoon we got a call from Bodean. He'd only been gone a few days, but already he sounded worldly wise. He told us all about the traffic jam they got stuck in on the way to Norfolk.

'It was bumper-to-bumper traffic,' he said wearily, as if it was something he'd been saying his whole life.

'How do you like Norfolk?' I asked.

'Oh, it's all right.' I could hear the restraint in his voice, as if he wanted to be excited but couldn't risk it. 'Last night we ordered a pizza, and they brought it right over in a box. I ate half of it by myself. If you don't believe me, ask my mama.'

'Are you homesick yet?'

'Do me a favor.'

'Come on, don't you miss me a little?'

'Make me an offer.' Then he said, 'My mama's got her own apartment. You ever been in an apartment?'

'No.'

'She's got a microwave oven and a dishwasher.'

'That's nice.'

'Yeah, I reckon I'll get me an apartment just as soon as I can.'

Flood came over and stood beside me, motioning to the phone. I was reluctant to hand it over to him. I was afraid he was going to tell Bodean about his new girlfriend. But Flood looked real eager, and I couldn't think of any way to stall.

'You want to talk to your daddy?' I asked Bodean.

'I reckon I might.'

I handed the receiver to Flood and braced myself for the worst.

'Hey, boy,' he said with a grin. 'I guess you're too good for us now.'

He just stood there listening, saying 'Uh-huh' now and then and laughing.

There was a pause, and then he said, 'Put your mama on for a second.'

I looked over at Papa who was sitting at the table with a bemused expression.

'Hey,' Flood said to Becky. 'Is he behaving himself? Well, don't let him run you ragged. He'll try to get away with murder . . . Yeah, we're all doing all right. Kind of quiet around here without him . . . Okay, well, you just send him home if he's too much trouble . . . No, just tell him I miss him. Everybody does.'

I swallowed a lump in my throat. Then Flood said good-bye and hung up. He stood there with his hand on the phone for a long time. Then he turned to me with a sigh.

'What are you looking at?' he asked.

'Nothing,' I said, but I must have been wearing my

feelings all over my face. It was the tone he used that got to me. He talked to Becky as if she was just an old acquaintance. There had been the slightest hint of affection in his voice, but it was the kind of tone he sometimes used when he was talking to me. It certainly wasn't the way a man should talk to a woman he was still in love with.

I went out and sat on the porch, feeling breathless and confused. The thing I just couldn't bring myself to believe was that it was all over. He could let her go as easily as that. All this time I thought he was waiting for her, he was really just holding a grudge. Now the grudge was gone, and there was nothing left at all. Nothing but the distant kind of bond between two people who used to be in love but weren't anymore.

It seemed impossible to me that love could evaporate like dew on a summer lawn. If love didn't stick around, then what did? Maybe Norma was right not to believe in anything. Maybe she knew that once you believed, you were bound to be disappointed.

After a few minutes Flood appeared on the porch. He stood next to me, and I could feel him looking at me, but I refused to raise my eyes. I heard him dragging a chair across the porch, and the next thing I knew his face was next to mine. He put his hand on my knee.

'You're upset with me,' he said.

'No, I'm not,' I lied.

'Well, I reckon you'll get used to the idea.'

'What idea?'

'Me and Lucy.'

I shuddered. 'That's your business, not mine.'

He laughed lightly. 'You always did love Becky. I got the feeling you liked her better than you liked me.'

'You're not going to marry her, are you?' I asked, meaning Becky, but he misunderstood.

'Maybe. I figure I better take it slow this time. That was where I messed up before.'

'Well,' I said, standing up, 'if you marry *that* woman you can forget about me ever speaking to you again.'

'Don't be like that, Dutch,' he said quietly. 'Don't get stuck in the past.'

'I'm not talking about the past.'

'Yes, you are, whether you know it or not. And another thing, you've got to let go of folks. You can't make them do what you want, any more than you can make it rain when you want it to. The world has got its own motion, Dutch, and the most you can do is just jump in there and try to ride along.'

'You're talking nonsense.'

Flood sighed, pressing his fingers together. 'I used to think you didn't have much Peyton blood in you. But now it's starting to come out.'

'What do you mean?'

'You sure expect a lot from people,' he explained. 'And you punish them when they don't live up to it.'

'That's a lie.'

'I saw Pop and Aunt Macy do it to Uncle Eugene. Never

could forgive him for being his own man. It wasn't that he left the farm in their hands. He couldn't have made that much difference even if he stayed behind. It's just that he chose another way. That's what they couldn't forgive.'

'Don't you talk about Papa,' I said, feeling tears spring to my eyes.

'He's a good man, I know that. As good as they get. But he's got expectations . . . he's got hard hopes. You've got them, too. Just don't let them get the best of you, that's all.'

'Sometimes I think you're going crazy.'

'I'm just giving you a little advice. Go easy on people.'

'I'll keep that in mind,' I said, though I had no intention of doing so. I intended to forget the whole conversation as soon as I could.

Then I turned and started walking, in no particular direction except away.

Twenty Six

My feet carried me down the road and into the woods. With each step I took a new vow to disown my brother. Just because I was related to him didn't mean I had to like him. And I certainly didn't have to believe the things he said.

But the trouble was, his words were nagging at me somewhere deep inside. Somehow I kept connecting them with Norma. I kept seeing her standing in the doorway of the bus, and I remembered the feeling I had when the doors closed and she disappeared. I'd suddenly known I liked her, and I couldn't understand why I hadn't seen it before. I had let her get away. I'd told myself it didn't matter because Norma was bad. But maybe she wasn't. Maybe she just wasn't the person I wanted her to be.

I had hard hopes, it was true. And now I understood why I was crying at the bus station and why I felt like crying when I heard Flood talking to Becky. Hard hopes hurt when they finally break apart.

When I came out of the woods, I was surprised to see that I had ended up at the church ball park. I was even more surprised to see that a softball game was in progress and that Ethan's team was in the outfield.

Well, that's what I was telling myself. Maybe I knew exactly where I was going and where I would end up.

As soon as the game was over, I thought about walking away. But I knew if I did that, I'd only be hoping that Ethan would see me and catch up with me. I figured I might as well make it easy on him. He saw me from halfway across the field and came over, walking fast at first and then slowing down when he saw that I wasn't leaving.

'Hey,' he said.

'Hi.'

'I didn't know you were coming.'

'I didn't either.'

'Did you see the whole game?'

'Just the last inning.'

'I hit a home run in the fifth.'

'I'm sorry I missed it.'

He shrugged. 'Well, it was really an error. They kept dropping the ball.'

'It still counts, though.'

'Yeah. But we still lost.'

'That's too bad.'

He nodded. He seemed to have run out of things to say.

'Well, I guess I'll be seeing you,' I said, starting to walk away.

'Where are you hurrying off to?'

'I don't know. I've got things to do.'

'Well, go do them then,' he snapped. 'Don't let me hang you up.'

'Okay.' I stared at him, then said, 'Ethan . . .'

'Let's just get one thing straight,' he said, interrupting me. 'What?'

He took a breath and let it out quickly. His face was flushed from the game, or maybe from something else, with little patches of red spreading across his cheeks.

He stared straight at me and said, 'Do you want to go with me?'

'Go with you where?'

He huffed and kicked at the grass. 'Steady, I mean.'

I was stunned. My mouth fell open and stayed there. Ethan didn't know what to make of that.

'If you don't want to, that's fine by me. I mean, if you're too *busy*. But I figured I might as well ask.'

'All right,' I said finally.

'All right what?'

'All right I will. Go with you, I mean.'

My heart was sinking a little. This wasn't the romantic moment I'd always dreamed of. But as moments went, it wasn't a bad one.

'Okay, then,' he said.

Now that it was decided, we both stood there wondering what came next. He looked down into his softball mitt and punched it with his fist.

'Well, then. I reckon I better walk you home.'

'You don't have to.'

'Yes, I do.'

'I mean, don't do me any favors.'

'Well, I want to.'

'Fine.'

We started walking together. I felt nervous now and had no idea what to say to him. I was starting to regret our decision. It was a lot easier to be with him before.

Ethan said, 'I guess we ought to get a few things straight then.'

'Like what?'

'Well, you should come to my softball games. And you should wear my cap when we're not in the field. That is, if you want to.'

I nodded. 'I could do that.'

'We should go to Bubba's together.'

'Now?'

'Not now. Fridays and Saturdays.'

'Okay.'

'Or we could go now if you want.'

'No, let's just walk.'

We walked in silence. I was so distracted that I almost didn't notice it was turning dark. I looked up to see why, and Ethan did, too. I sucked in my breath when I saw a big blue cloud covering the sun.

'Look!' I said.

'I see it.'

We stood there staring up at the sky. There was more than one cloud. They were moving fast and bunching together. A warm wind stirred around us.

'It looks like the real thing,' Ethan said.

214

'Wow,' was all I could think to say.

We started walking again. I kept waiting to feel rain, but it didn't come. Still, I could smell it . . . a damp, musty smell like a basement in winter.

Ethan said, 'Think we should hold hands?'

'Yeah, probably.'

He took my hand. My palm was sweating but so was his. I liked the way my hand seemed to get swallowed up in his. I smiled up at him, but he looked straight ahead.

Maybe this was how Becky and Flood had walked together once, hand in hand, smiling as they thought about all the things that could happen. I wondered if they had lost that somehow, if one day they woke up and decided not to be in love. Or maybe it slipped away as quietly as a cat, almost without their seeing it. They just turned, and it was gone.

I felt a quick flash of panic as I studied Ethan's face. Would that happen to us? Would things suddenly turn sour? I couldn't stand the idea of him just letting go of me, turning on me . . . or maybe even hating me. The chance that everything could go wrong was like a monster, following you around, breathing down your neck. In an instant I understood what Aunt Macy meant when she talked about the other side of love. And I knew without a doubt that it was a struggle to stay on the good side. Love wasn't always light and breezy, the way I had imagined. It was big and messy. It was a hard, heavy feeling and it pressed down on me.

Was that why Becky and Flood gave up . . . and Norma's parents, too? Was it that they couldn't stand the weight?

It was a whole different ballgame now that love was a real possibility, with two actual people involved, not just something I'd dreamed about while lying on my bed. The whole thing scared me so that I wanted to put a stop to it then and there. But I thought about what Flood said, how the world has its own motion. You couldn't resist it. You just had to close your eyes and dive in and wait to see where it took you.

I looked up at the sky. It was a dark blue, almost purple. The air was swollen and damp. And the whole universe felt swollen with possibilities.

Ethan suddenly stopped walking and put his arm around me.

'Listen,' he said.

I did. It was quiet, a deep, soft silence that spread all around us. But then, in the distance there was a faint rumble, like a faraway train.

'Thunder,' Ethan whispered.

It came again, louder this time, followed by a flash of light. Then the rain came, big hot drops of water plopping down on our faces. The ground hissed and sizzled with gratitude. Ethan and I just stared at each other as the rain started to fall in sheets. We were soaked to the skin, and I felt a little bit embarrassed, the way you feel when you wake up and discover that someone has been watching you sleep.

'Can I kiss you?' he asked.

'Will you stop *asking*? You're supposed to just do it.'

He kissed me so hard I felt the circulation cutting off in my lips. I was starting to think I might suffocate when he stopped.

'How was that?' he asked.

'Terrible.'

He shrugged and smiled, his eyes squinting shut and raindrops running like tears down his cheeks.

'It'll get better,' he said.

ORDER FORM

New to the Signature Series:

0 340 70965 0	The Apostle Bird	£4.99	❐
0 340 71661 4	A Secret Place	£4.99	❐
0 340 68127 6	Blackthorn, Whitethorn	£4.99	❐
0 340 71600 2	Skellig	£4.99	❐
0 340 65679 4	Midnight Fair	£4.99	❐
0 340 70902 2	The Story Collector	£4.99	❐
0 340 65147 4	Undercurrents	£4.99	❐

All Hodder Children's books are available at your local bookshop, or can be ordered direct from the publisher. Just tick the titles you would like and complete the details below. Prices and availability are subject to change without prior notice.

Please enclose a cheque or postal order made payable to *Bookpoint Ltd*, and send to: Hodder Children's Books, 39 Milton Park, Abingdon, OXON OX14 4TD, UK. Email Address: orders@bookpoint.co.uk

If you would prefer to pay by credit card, our call centre team would be delighted to take your order by telephone. Our direct line *01235 400414* (lines open 9.00 am–6.00 pm Monday to Saturday, 24 hour message answering service). Alternatively you can send a fax on *01235 400454*.

TITLE		FIRST NAME		SURNAME	
ADDRESS					
DAYTIME TEL:			POST CODE		

If you would prefer to pay by credit card, please complete:
Please debit my Visa/Access/Diner's Card/American Express (delete as applicable) card no:

Signature ....

Expiry Date: ....

If you would NOT like to receive further information on our products please tick the box. ❐